CHAPTERS AND VERSE

CHAPTERS AND VERSE

JOEL BARR

PEREGRINE SMITH BOOKS
SALT LAKE CITY

First edition
92 91 90   5 4 3 2 1

This is a Peregrine Smith Book, published by
Gibbs Smith, Publisher
P.O. Box 667
Layton, Utah 84041

This is a work of fiction and all the characters are fictional. Any similarities to persons living or dead are purely coincidental.

Design by Randall Smith
Cover illustration by Susette Billedeaux

Manufactured in the United States of America

Library of Congress Cataloging-in-Publication Data

Barr, Joel. 1946-
    Chapters and verse / Joel Barr.
         p.   cm.
    ISBN 0-87905-340-2 (pbk.)
    I. Title
PS3552.A731835C4 1991
813' .54--dc20   90-46242
                                      CIP

91 — 2518

For Abby, for Aaron

CHAPTERS AND VERSE

> *You don't just put up with interruptions around here.*
> *You live for them. Interruptions are the business.*
>
> E BAKER

CHAPTER

1

Photography, Art, Biography A–L, Biography M–Z, Travel. Then a right and a jog past Fiction, Fiction, Fiction, Fiction to a lone gondola marked Mostly History. It isn't.

Unlike the rest of the store, Mostly History is just a bit off. You can't argue titles into or out of the section. Here the current status of the Chinese Revolution shares equal billing with a history of the medical profession, a two-volume summary of ecological disasters in the Northeast, and a pictorial analysis of Central American geopolitics. Here is the only shelf in the store devoted to the Old West and another which probably contains everything in print about the Japanese tourist. John McPhee lives here. So does Richard Selzer. You can't go to this section for something in particular. You come here to search for surprises and to be discovered by a book.

Like several of our regulars, Thad Collins feels that someone plants books there for him alone. Maybe. Thad rations his visits. He only calls on Mostly History when he has a gift to buy. Today he's looking for a present for his new friend, Ramsey Wills. They struck up a conversation three Saturdays ago and the two of them left together discussing an LBJ biography and a Nancy comic book. Thad was arguing that the two books had equal social significance and that their respective protagonists contributed equally to the lives of the populace. I didn't hear the full rebuttal, but it had something to do with men and power. Thad was pressing the case for women and endurance as the two left the store.

Today, reviewing the titles on the eight shelves of strange bookfellows, Thad seems to be visualizing Ramsey's face as he receives each book. Thad will probably spend half an hour skimming books,

1

hefting them, gazing upward, replacing them and selecting others. When he finally makes a selection, it will be with a look that conveys the "yes, yes" of a wise scientist in a forties movie who, with one sniff of a vial, has discovered both the secret of life and the evil intentions of his lab assistant.

If Thad wants to choose what Ramsey chooses himself, he'll move to the poetry section. Ramsey usually buys modern-poetry anthologies, never illustrated ones. Thad seems to be settling on a photo essay about Northern Ireland. I think he's making a mistake but, then again, there's a lot of misreading at Chapters and Verse.

When I took over Chapters and Verse a year ago, I inherited a small storage cabinet filled with bookstoreabilia. It took me a year to decide to look through the folders and papers on the shelves because they weren't germane to the store itself, and the materials seemed still to belong to my predecessor, E Baker. It was only after I'd read and reread her last letter that it seemed appropriate to take a look at everything.

Consistent with the compulsive behavior nurtured by years in a store full of carefully categorized books, each of the three shelves in the cabinet contained its own class of abilia. The lowest shelf was full of awards. E had apparently saved every award she had earned since grade school. In her sixty or more years, she had created a sizeable plaque, trophy, and certificate library as a private monument to herself. As I emptied this shelf, honor by honor, onto the desk, E Baker took shape out of the calligraphy and brass as a selective, determined achiever.

From her preschool years, a fringed red ribbon proclaimed her membership in the Hartford Numbers Club: A Club for Very Young Ladies Who Have Learned to Count. A scroll which I couldn't flatten proclaimed that our Miss Baker had completed something called Early Elocution. Another scroll expressed the gratitude of a Connecticut senator for E's generous contribution to the Connecticut Children's Settlement for Unfortunate Parentless Children. As far as I could tell, our heroine counted beautifully, spoke well, and had a heart of gold before she turned six.

When she hit grade school, E went to her strengths. For three years running, she won the Wilson School Math Award for her class. She studied piano. The dollar or two her folks paid for each lesson must have included recital and ribbon fees, since she kept red and blue ribbons as mementos of her virtuosity on the keyboard at the Spring Recital for Family and Friends.

E also joined a group called the Voices of Norwich, which awarded her with three certificates for attendance. The symbol of the Voices, a crossed pitchfork and violin, suggested that the club was dedicated to agrarian music. One certificate was signed on the back by fellow Voices with notes like, "Play on EB," or "Remember your handkerchief, young lady," or "Maylynn and Pearl are behind you." I'll bet she laughed when she first read these notes.

Somewhere around twelve years of age, E either stopped being involved in awardable activities, stopped deserving recognition, or stopped saving her awards. The shelf offered nothing about the next few years except a certificate of completion of the ninth grade, to which was clipped a Special Notation of Excellence in Field Hockey. We can only guess what she went through in those difficult years when she was looking down at a new body, looking around at others looking around at her, and trying to figure out why she was so miserable when everyone else was so popular and happy. Since no one in history has ever done anything of note from ages twelve through fifteen, there is no reason to be harsh with E Baker for taking these years off.

She came back strong in high school as a thespian. Stenciled playbills highlighted an illustrious and progressive career on the stage, during which she progressed from doing set work and being a sailor in *Major Tapps Meets Ensign Simon* to a supporting role as a horse-race caller in *Can Carinda Canter?* That play was written by an Edwin Baker, perhaps a pseudonym. Finally, E got the lead role of Milady in a musical comedy called *Chaos and Love Come to Bay Meadow*, a three-act play with, according to the program, only one intermission.

Along with the playbills, E amassed seven certificates for Honors List grades, one trophy for Girls Broad Jump, Open Competition, a brass lamp inscribed "Lamplighters, E Baker and Tam Shands," and the only graduation certificate I've ever seen with the principal's picture printed above his signature. She also won a plaque recognizing her tutoring efforts with the girls of St. Margaret's Day School. Pasted to the back of the plaque was a brown photograph of a smiling girl of seven or eight who had signed her name, Patty, below the words "Don't graduate, please."

E attended a private college called Weston which showed a Waterbury address on her diploma. Her degree was a Bachelor of Arts in Arts, a bumbling sort of title which is as purposefully nonspecific as any other degree. No other record of her college years was on the shelf, so I learned little more about this period in the life of the mysterious woman who was never referred to by any name fuller than E Baker.

Her life as an adult was shelved in two phases. The first I call her narrating period. Out of college she took a series of jobs which required her to tell people about things. These were documented in papers assembled in a cardboard box of the type used to collect a year's worth of magazines. A reference letter from an early supervisor praised her work as an orientation specialist in the naval-recruiting office. I could see her explaining to new recruits the travel they could expect, the type of ships they'd be manning, or the order of rank and the saluting responsibilities they'd face. I doubted that she would say much about the food, barracks, and "real" life the recruits were most interested in, but I'll bet she was serious about presenting the facts of their enlistment. Copies of resignation letters showed that she had also worked for five years as a tour guide at a number of state historic sites, and for eight as a reporter and copy editor for a weekly paper in Danbury. She had also won a commendation letter for her work as a community relations officer for the Connecticut State Police.

Somewhere near the end of her narrating period, E moved from Connecticut to Florida. This in itself isn't unusual since people in Connecticut are liable to move to Florida most anytime. E worked as a reference librarian in Orlando and saved To Whom It May Concern letters from her library superiors when she left four years later. They cited her tenacity in searching out facts.

She must have been about forty when she moved to Tangelo to open her bookstore. I would have been in the second or third grade at Tangelo Elementary, probably making pilgrims' heads out of construction paper and preposterous excuses for not finishing homework.

With the establishment of Chapters and Verse, E entered her second phase of adulthood, which I call her character phase because she called it that. The entrance to this new period, one in which she was working for herself for the first time, was

4

momentous for her. It was so important, in fact, that she decided to honor herself for making a courageous and drastic change. She hand-lettered a Certificate of Lifelong Importance for herself, in which she offered a lofty "Whereas: E Baker has, after years of study, patience, watching, serving, and wishing, taken a step in the downhill of her life which she realizes to be unusual and entirely special . . ."

The certificate then proclaimed her a "True and Legitimate Character of the Town" and recognized the uniqueness of her ways. E Baker, like many of the authors she promoted, apparently felt the need to document her individuality. She signed her own certificate in a defiant, confident hand and, according to oral histories I've collected, immediately set about earning the title she had bestowed upon herself.

Acquaintances attested to her unique character with statements like the following:

"She dressed funny and didn't know it."

"E Baker was fearless. She didn't know she wasn't supposed to speak her mind no matter what."

"Silent? Never. She had opinions on every book in the place, every author, every article in every magazine. She must have read like a demon."

"She was almost crazy. The store was sort of a pen in which she bounced around, scowling and laughing and always telling people to read, read. 'You don't know everything,' she'd say, 'so read this little novel and come back and tell me what you think.' When people came back to tell her, she'd listen, argue a bit, and thank them for talking with her about the book. Then, from under the counter, she'd pull out a book she'd been saving just for this person and offer it as a gift along with a smile which deserved an award."

"Money didn't matter to E. She seemed to have principles and pride which carried her along. But she never preached. I never knew anyone so sure that what she was doing was proper."

"She made more people read more books than any teacher. Her excitement about books was sort of infectious. How could you leave E's bookstore without a book you had to start reading immediately?"

"She lived alone, I think. No one ever asked her about herself and got an answer he or she could write down. She learned more about them from their questions than they learned about her from her answers. I liked her. I remember her very clearly. There was nothing halfway about E Baker."

These statements weren't on the cabinet shelf, of course. They were out in the town. The shelf did hold several plaques from the various local schools for her work with them on book fairs, library building programs, and reading contests. A letter from the owner of WTAN thanked her for nine years of book reviews, done faithfully each Saturday morning, including the time "you looked so ill with the flu that your notes seemed too heavy for you to manage." There were another twenty or more plaques and certificates thanking E or her store for this or that contribution.

The woman attracted recognition, and if she didn't leave behind a row of books—like some authors—she did leave her autobiography on these shelves.

Corb Sams is in and holding court between Travel and Crafts. He has his usual entourage of two: Irv Tyson, the only man in town to have retired wealthy at thirty with a fabled fortune from phosphate mining, and a woman I don't know who's often with the other two and usually shaking her head in amazement at Corb. Corb is fairly loud when he's on and, as far as I've seen, he's always on. Customers who aren't used to hearing him often frown in his direction, trying to locate the bellowing and pontificating. The frowns usually go away when they realize they have a world-class pontificator in their midst.

Corb isn't tall, handsome, deep voiced, or muscular. Still, like any leading man, he comes complete with followers, absolute self-confidence, and an unfailing ploy for grabbing the spotlight even when there's no stage. Corb reduces every problem, task, book, or author to a maxim. He produces a brief statement of truth so clever and memorable that it takes over from the subject itself and becomes part of the permanent lexicon of everyone in the room:

"One war, one treaty."
"Never set a secret plan loose in the forest when the leaves are dry."

6

"Books about Spain are always full of errors."

"Everything works on lawyers except bluff."

"Some people fight just to fight. Help them find each other."

"Nobody ever wrote the truth about Korea because nobody wanted to know."

"There are only two kinds of novels: novels which tell a story and bad novels."

He seems to arrive instantly at these nuggets in lightning jags through his synapses which defy the plodding, rational road the rest of us take. His one-liners come out involuntarily, it seems, at the very moment of their conception. Corb himself seems to stand back and marvel at his work.

If Corb is unmatched in his prowess with the original maxim, it isn't because he hones his skills with lessons from the masters. I've never seen him even browse through Twain, Mencken, Hotchner, or Alexander Pope. He even seems to work his magic without Dr. Johnson. In fact, when Corb comes up to the front to check out, his selections are completely disconnected from his eternal road show. He reads everything written by William Goldman and often buys more than one copy of a title. He says he reads the same work from different starting points using different copies so he can check for consistency. Why Goldman gets so much of Corb's attention, I don't know. When he doesn't buy Goldman, he reads Jerome Weidman or books about sports psychology. Except for one week when he bought everything we had by Charles Webb, he hasn't varied his choices. To listen to him, though, you'd think he'd be reading from every section in the place. Maybe he sneak reads or maybe, though I hate to think it, he's in a mail-order book club.

Irv Tyson usually buys three or four paperbacks and thereby qualifies as a "stocker"—someone who buys books like bread, a week's supply at a time. He usually buys doctor novels. These are novels which, I maintain, have long deserved to be called genre novels, like romances or westerns, since they all have the same setting and plot. Young Doctor Warren begins practice in a hospital with overbearing senior staff, an incredible overload of cases and exotic diseases, a nurse, patient, or administrator who obviously will be the romantic interest, and a set of ideals that just won't quit. Despite adversity the senior staff is tamed, the rare diseases are conquered, the romantic interest becomes interested, and the ideals just don't

7

quit. Full of surprises, those medical types. Dr. Warren would never sing in a sun shower.

The woman reads most anything that comes in a series. She's plowed through Piers Anthony, the Oz books, all four of the Hitchhiker Trilogy, and shelves full of mystery series. John Jakes kept her going a good while in our tall-ships years. The subject doesn't matter; she seems interested only in matching her reading persistence with authors who have earned her respect by plugging on and on.

What fascinates me about this group is their balance. When three people do anything together on a regular basis for any length of time, it is noteworthy. Most sports require two people. Others need five, nine, or eleven, but none that I can think of uses three people on a side. Classes are usually larger than three people, car pools seem to favor four riders, and couples always come in twos. Somehow this group works, at least for book-buying forays. My theory is that Corb's continuous and clever chatter is matched by Irv Tyson's leisure to listen and complimented by the mystery woman's wonder at prolonged wordsmithing. Take away any one of them, and either there's no speaker, no listener, or no corroborating witness. Add one and somebody's out of a job.

The balance was temporarily threatened last week when Irv showed Corb Giles Goat Boy and proudly announced, "That's how you repeat a good idea to death." Corb nodded, without smiling, and returned to his browsing with a slight tightening of his lips. The woman overheard, of course, and looked back and forth at the faces of the two men to see what would come next. A few minutes later, Corb suddenly became a John Barth defender and retaliated with three Robert B. Parker mysteries and the solemn commentary, "This is how you get a good idea about repeated deaths." All sides of the triangle were pleased.

The middle shelf of the storage cabinet contained display props used in the front window over the years. It was the only shelf I felt right in exploring until recently. There was quite an odd assemblage of stuff on it, which I bagged and took home to ponder. Eventually the bag became the focus of a parlor game for my friends and me. We'd pull out a prop and challenge each other to place books which had featured it in the window. Each window had to have at least ten titles, and only when the window was filled could we go on to another prop. Subtlety was an absolute requirement of our game, unlike day-to-day retailing, in which sales and cleverness are inversely related.

Fish of Florida or *The Sportsman's Guide to Fishing the Flats*, for example, could not be placed in a window with the fishing tackle box found in the bag. More suitable titles would be *Fear of Fly Fishing, A Farewell to Worms, The Carp Is a Lonely Hunter*, and anything by Alison Lurie. We did quite well with most of the props, things like bow ties, valentines, and turkey cutouts, but never finished a window to go with an old mason jar full of buttons.

The cabinet's top shelf was the legal shelf. It held the corporate books, a metal embossing instrument with the corporate seal on it, and an empty binder labeled "Corporate Minutes," which I thought would be a terrific book title. There was also a hand-labeled manila folder for "Legal Papers." The folder held a yellowed Fictitious Name Notice announcing to the world that Chapters and Verse was doing business at its Suwannee Road address, and that the party responsible for that name and activity was an E Baker, President, Books of Character, Inc., a Florida corporation.

Besides the notice, there was only a single sheet of paper in the folder, kept over the years by E for reasons only she would know. It listed the various names she had considered for the store and her comments on each.

Names for Store

1. Leaves—subtle, misleading?, flowery

2. Page After Page—makes reading seem tedious

3. READ HERE—certainly to the point, I like it, no one else will

4. Bookshelf, Bookworm, Book Bin, Book Center, Book anything—too many of these things around

5. Read 'em and Weep—cute but rules out many types of books, great for a section of romances

6. Baker Books—good for ego, too good for ego, sounds like a cookbook store

7. Town Books—boring, boring

8. Browsers—close but sounds like a dog's name

9. The Bibliophile—will keep some people away, never do that

10. In Print—might be confused with a printer's shop but best so far

11. Read Any Good Books Lately?—risque?

12. Not-a-Chain Bookstore—sounds a little like sour grapes, okay for a bigger city

13. Books for All—No. Please!

14. Look It Up—not bad, better for a library, a little haughty

15. Chapters and Verse—gives equal weight to verse, the world doesn't, keep thinking

16. Can't Put It Down—ambiguous

17. Spine Out—only insiders would know

18. Today's Titles—alliteration is okay, these words aren't

19. Authors' House—consider this one

NO SOLICITING. This notice includes little children who may profess not to understand it and who look most needful in their band uniforms, Little League hats, or scout shirts. It also includes parents of these young solicitors who just know we wouldn't mind making an exception for their child.

E BAKER

CHAPTER

2

Our store is half a block from a small hotel—a refurbished inn which cares a great deal about its service, flowers, glass, brass, and oak. It makes its way by accommodating visiting celebrities, tourists who tire of slick look-alike motels, and salesmen who want a change of pace and a downtown to walk in after dinner. The Windsor also hosts an occasional conference and this week its WELCOME VISITORS TO THE WINDSOR letter board announces the Third Annual Florida Conference on Helping Professionals.

That's good. Social workers, counselors, and the like love to read and we've beefed up our psychology and self-help sections. But that name, Helping Professionals . . .

It might as well be a convention of trust-department managers, tractor designers, or insurance people. Surely they see themselves as helping professionals as well. Face it, we are all good people, sell a good product, help others make out. What's life without a car, a car without a bumper? What kind of economy would we have without typists or paper-bag makers? And who's to say who's being helped and who's the helper, or which social worker could just as earnestly sell mutual funds?

Several jobs before I met E Baker and bought Chapters and Verse, I was a social worker for the state. I didn't have a caseload like my colleagues, though. Instead I was an arbiter of benefits. Caseworkers were supposed to apply eligibility criteria to their prospective clients to see if they qualified for money, food stamps, day-care vouchers, or other necessities. When the caseworkers were stumped or afraid to make a decision, they came to me.

At twenty-three, with a new Master of Social Policy degree as meaningful as E's Bachelor of Arts in Arts, I was deciding whether a family of eight deserved help with their food bill or whether an elderly widower qualified as legally blind under Section 229.2, subpart III. As proprietor of a secondary way station on the road to benefits which I always felt to be well deserved, I defined my "arbitration" as justification. If there was any way I could contrive a favorable decision on benefits, I would do it. When an outside audit of my bureau revealed that of 225 decisions in two years, I'd favored the client on 205, I was tactfully encouraged to move on.

I quit to travel the South. I would contribute to social justice by preparing a photo essay about rural poverty. Somewhere along the line, this Walker Evans was transformed into a confused film waster for whom everything and everyone had nobility. I must have thought I had discovered a new soul in America's southern farmlands. Sadly my photography and writing were amateurish, so I couldn't market my discovery. I came home and sold neckties at the minimall.

Business came easy: few rules to read, few meetings to attend, no reports to write, and no questioning of eligibility to participate. Best of all, there was, given basic honesty, little in the way of imponderable moral dilemmas. Some people even smiled when I helped them pick a tie. I was coasting.

During my stint at Nathan's Tie One On, I came into some money in the great American tradition. A childless uncle and aunt died together and bequeathed all their belongings and savings to me and to the local chapter of the Save the Florida Cross-State Barge Canal Association. The association had been disbanded some fifteen years before Aunt Pearl and Uncle Charles finally gave their gift, so everyone figured that they had simply forgotten to update their will.

Somehow lost in the discussion over their strange intended bequeathment was the question of why I had been chosen, from among their brothers, sisters, and three other nephews, to receive the inheritance. I would have been, after all, only about nine years old when the will was prepared. Everyone shrugged, however, and, by their silence, awarded me my share as well as the share that would have gone to the association dedicated to setting adrift Florida's southern half. I convinced myself that I was a better bet anyway, and accepted the kindness.

My selection became a mystery and a responsibility for me. Why had I been chosen? Had I once said something or done something quite meaningful or portentous for my aunt and uncle? Had they hired someone to film my reaction? For what anticipated deeds had I been given financial backing?

Since my own future was far from clear, and my past was a zigzag of bureaucratic maneuvering, questionable photography, and attempts to match accessories with three-piece suits, I spent a few months doing a grass-is-greener survey. Every time I heard people say "I always wanted to . . . ," I wrote down their wishes. I kept the tally in a journal I was writing at the time. It ran like this:

". . . quit working for two to three years and travel" 3

". . . work part-time and write part-time" 1

". . . go back to school in music" 1

". . . go back to school in business" 2

". . . go back to school in North Carolina" 4

". . . do something in the dark with Lorraine Thompson" 1

". . . buy a pinball machine" 1

". . . spend two weeks on a fat farm" 1

". . . open a bookstore" 6

". . . open a restaurant" 3

". . . open a coffeehouse" 3

". . . open a wine and cheese shop" 6

". . . chuck it all and drift" 2

". . . spend a year deciding what to do" 4

I worry now about this last group because they seem to have no dreams at the ready. I might have been one of these people as well, but, in truth, I was one of the 1's above, though not the Lorraine Thompson admirer. I never considered a bookstore, even after my survey was completed. E Baker and the bookstore somehow found me.

"What have you signed up for so far?" The counselor looked somewhat younger, if a little more tired, than the student. They were sitting on the floor by the health books.

The student, a dark-haired girl of nineteen who "really did want input," jiggled a key ring featuring a plastic breakfast and a tiny Betty Boop. "Fear and Anxieties. The one with the book, not the one where you pair off and write journals at each other. And I'm taking Child Abuse and probably The Man in Women's Literature. I'm worried about all the reading and papers. What do you think?"

"I think you're trapping yourself a bit. Why not ease up some? I suggest Art History. You need something like that to let grad schools know you're after a liberal education."

"I was thinking about that. Either Art History or Forensic Psych." The plastic eggs settled on the top of her wrist, sunny-side down. "I thought Forensic Psych might help if I'm going into advertising. I'd like to know how what I say impacts the market. You know."

The counselor spoke slowly, kindly. "Forensic Psychology isn't forensics like speech. It's a, well, sort of a guidance course for psychologists who have to testify in court. It doesn't seem like it's right for you, but still, I've never met a psych prof I didn't like."

"Didn't somebody say that?" asked the student, seeking more input.

"Will Rogers said something like that."

"Will Rogers?"

"Don't you know who he was?"

"No," was the honest answer of the dejected student.

"He was a comedian. Kind of like Lincoln."

"Oh," said the student with reverence.

They arranged to meet again at the store after a week had passed and the student could think more about her course schedule.

Magazines are like elephants. More people would rather look at them than get involved with them, and nobody knows where they go when they die.

CORB SAMS

CHAPTER

3

Not long after I started to work at Nathan's Tie One On, every day turned into a Wednesday. I knew my work there had to end, but I couldn't quite see where I would be going next.

There is nothing more terrifying than the thought that your parents and teachers were right when they bleated over and over that "you can do anything you want to do." No sentence ever uttered carries such baggage. I had determination, technique, experience and now, thanks to Uncle Charles and Aunt Pearl, capital. I had a survey to tell me what my fellow searchers would do if they had their choice. I was primed, hungry, in shape, and floundering.

One Wednesday, Wade Hamstead came in to find a tie for a suit he'd just bought to wear at the wedding of his boss's son. Wade was telling me how his boss had given all his employees a bonus to buy wedding clothes to assure good attendance at the ceremony and how bad that made them feel. He was up to the point of describing what a hapless fellow the son was to begin with, when a woman walked in.

She was wearing a hat. Since no one wore hats around here, unless they wore ball caps or were E Baker, I assumed it was her. E Baker owned Chapters and Verse. She *was* Chapters and Verse, from what I had heard. Her hat featured some grapes, cherries, and assorted other fruits which I had only seen on hats worn by Minnie Pearl or women who were butts of jokes in Three Stooges or Marx Brothers' movies. However E Baker was not, according to her reputation, one to mimic herself. She was one to merit attention and didn't seem to mind being talked about. On her that hat was as natural as a blousy, open-collar shirt on a poet, a bow tie on a cellist, or a maroon bolo tie with silver tips and a fish clip on a rancher.

While I listened to Wade carry on about how the boss wanted them all to come out to his house to see the lake after the wedding, and how a suggested present list had been posted in the employees' lounge with the note "They really don't need any art work," E Baker began to eavesdrop. No, that's not quite fair. In a small-town tie store, there isn't a lot of room, so any conversation is public record and Wade was not concerned about who heard his rambling. Still I could see E inching closer and could tell that she had begun studying my face as I listened to Wade's story.

It is hard to act naturally when someone you don't know is studying your face. You feel flattered, wet under the arms, and under pressure to be quite appealing. I scratched my cheek, tried a smile, and remembered with some embarrassment why I had never met E. Strange as it may seem today, I had never been in her store, though I was, of course, a reader. I was a library regular rather than a buyer. I had stopped buying books after college since I hated having to move them from place to place as I tried to do the various anythings I thought I wanted to do. Besides, I lived several miles from downtown Tangelo and had little reason to drive in to shop.

E was in her early sixties on that Wednesday afternoon. Her face, however, seemed to be in its midforties with no signs of aging further. I had learned to read faces long before from my father. He told me that in every man I could find a little boy's face fighting to stay out front. In children, he said, could be found the face they would have seventy years later if I stretched the forehead and brought the cheeks up and eyes down. Women showed their age in their eyes, and my father said that each instance of pain and happiness in their lives was recorded in the iris and in the folds of skin that surround the eye. His guidelines were general but he started me in the right direction.

E's eyes said little about happiness and nothing about weariness. Instead they were the eyes I identify with the candidate who's been on the road for months and is still going strong. Hers were the eyes of the executive who works eighteen hours a day, catching only catnaps, fighting for achievement of this or that at a pace which most people can sustain only for short periods. Her face presented a woman who had much to do, who always had much to do, and who showed no signs of tiring and gave no hint of complaint.

She had picked out a tie almost immediately upon coming in, but she seemed not to want to hurry Wade along. I offered to ring her up while he was deciding but she waved me off and continued staring at me.

After Wade made his selection and finally left, E presented her tie for purchase. I feared she was going to say something personal and difficult to handle, like how I looked like a son she had lost in the war, or how she had once danced with a boy like me and wondered if I could waltz. If young men are most ignorant about any one thing, surely it must be the thoughts and feelings of older women.

Instead of asking me anything difficult, she made her purchase and asked me to wrap the tie. While I was fighting the white tissue paper into the box, E continued studying me and finally asked what types of books I liked to read. The question was an obvious red herring in the tie store, but it didn't surprise me. I explained that I read mostly biographies and novels. She asked me how I made choices between novels, which biographies I remembered best, and what I was reading at the time. I was pleased to be able to tell her honestly that I was reading an excellent biography of Faulkner. Like a psychiatrist listening to symptoms, E nodded and withheld judgment. She suggested I read some books on science or world history to surprise myself from time to time and said she'd pull some books for me to consider. As if I were a regular at her store, I said I'd look at them next time I was in.

She left but returned ten minutes later. She walked up to me at the counter and said, "Matthew Mason, I like the way you listen to people." She left again without waiting for me to respond.

She knew my name. Probably she had asked next door, but she knew my name. I still don't know what made her think I was a more patient listener than the next guy, but I had never been so flattered. When a person of such obvious strength and confidence sees something special in you, the promise in the world becomes exciting and the choices no longer terrifying. We all need so little to fill up with hope and anticipation. I

17

found myself wondering how long I should wait before going to her store.

Because the other worker at Nathan's got sick, I couldn't get to the bookstore during the following week. As each day passed, I began to get mad at myself for spending my time in a world limited to forty-two-inch-long strips of cloth that men wrapped around their necks to make themselves acceptable and uncomfortable in the presence of other men who were similarly irritated.

I began rehearsing what I would say to E when I finally walked into Chapters and Verse:

"So. Let's see the books you're sure will change my reading habits."
"One person's ties are another person's books."
"Let me look around for a while and then I'd like to see those books on science you mentioned."
"Oh. I see you have that Faulkner book I told you about."

By the end of the week, my opening lines had changed:

"Sorry I couldn't get in earlier. I wanted to finish the Faulkner biography first."
"I was digesting a couple of books before I was ready to tackle some new things."
"Do you remember me from the tie store?"

E Baker came to see me before I could get to Chapters and Verse. She brought with her a copy of *The Starship and the Canoe*, which she placed in front of me and never mentioned. Instead she asked me if I'd like to come work with her as store manager.

I was used to jobs being sought and offered with conventional advertisements, application forms, résumés, interviews, delays, callbacks, and various other forms of sparring. E just didn't work that way and her brashness dared me to keep up. I began questioning myself as to whether I should get involved with anyone as obviously impulsive as E Baker, but then I thought, "She has chosen me. How bad can her judgment be?"

18

While I answered her in as steady a voice as I could, "I have to give Nathan two weeks," I realized that we had not discussed my new responsibilities, hours, or salary, and that I had never been in my new place of employment. E knew what she wanted, I was it, and therefore I wanted it, too. My years of college, my experience in government, photography, and tie selling notwithstanding, I was taking a job with a woman I barely knew who wanted me because, presumably, I listened well. If she could be impulsive, so could I.

Facing each other over a showcase filled with green ties— St. Patrick's Day was a week away—E Baker and I shook hands, looked at the startled expression on each other's faces, and started to laugh.

In our business you can't set your own prices. For the most part, you can't negotiate your cost of goods, either. You can't easily go into manufacturing for yourself to increase profits, and you certainly can't get huffy with a supplier and threaten to take your business elsewhere. ("I'll just go buy the latest Michener novel from some other publisher while you work on your pricing and customer-relations program!") You don't have the potential to make the proverbial killing in a single season, because even a $15.95 blockbuster which sells three hundred copies results in a gross profit under $2,000 and blockbusters are as common as good child actors. About the only thing we booksellers have in common with real businesses is our right to complain.

So, we look for sidelines.

I'm a righteous, merchantly, literary purist in my selection of these nonbook items which, we all know in the industry, allow for HUGE markups and quick profits. I've allowed only book-related sidelines in the store—no puzzles or koalas for me. I inherited this bias from E, who paces about in my brain muttering that booksellers should sell books or change their profession. Though I've remained steadfast in my criteria, I've almost always chosen losers.

Among the worst of my choices:

T-shirts with the Bloomsbury Group on them. ("Is this Mozart or somebody?")

Brass bookmarks with authors' heads embossed on them. (Only Dickens sold well because his likeness was confused somehow for that of John Lennon.)

19

Posters featuring famous opening lines even I couldn't place. (Where was Sister Carita when I needed her?)

Stuffed animals ranging from sea gulls (These arrived three months after Jonathan Livingston fell from the bestsellers' lists.) to dressed rabbits. (Nobody seemed to care too much about Beatrix Potter's birthday.)

The absolute worst of my selections was packs of collectors' author cards similar to baseball cards. I had such high hopes for these. After all, people will collect anything. Besides, parents could use them to lure children to culture. Teachers could use them for rewards. When I heard about them, I couldn't believe my luck. No other store in town had them. I couldn't wait for them to come in.

They arrived with their own display—a cardboard floor dump designed to practically hand these gems, at fifty-nine cents a package, to lines of eager collectors. People aggressively ignored the entire display. Looking back, I'm sure it was because the makers, a company called Culture Chew, selected licorice-flavored chewing gum to include in each pack and proclaimed as much in bold letters at the top of the display.

I still own a complete set of English poets, American mystery writers, and the Shakespeare All-Star series. I never could get a Tennessee Williams card.

Nonfiction is fiction which the author believes to be true.

CORB SAMS

CHAPTER

4

E Baker hadn't told the whole truth. I knew this because she told me so at five thirty in the morning about a week after I gave notice to Nathan. She called on a Saturday, rushing me through a favorite dream in which I was teaching myself to be a sculptor, and woke me up with the classic, "Did I wake you?"

My hands were still testing the surface of the telephone receiver, reviewing its contours for a modernistic masterpiece capturing commercial functionalism in bronze, when my mind caught up with her question. I answered just like everyone does when someone wakes them up. "No, you didn't wake me up. It's actually good you called. I needed to get up anyway."

"I didn't tell you everything about you and me and the store. I need to. When can we discuss it? I eat breakfast at Anson's at seven."

It was unnecessary for her to add the customary questions about whether seven at Anson's was convenient, whether I needed directions, or whether I had any questions about the immediate need for a meeting. Our two previous discussions had been completely without the politic and guile of normal conversation, and this early-morning one was the same.

At six thirty I found myself driving on Suwannee Road toward the downtown business district. For the first time I could remember, I was driving through my hometown in daylight with no other cars to hurry me along, no neon to snarl at me to do this or that, and a destination that promised a completely unpredictable meeting.

The blocks of houses and oaks presented themselves on each side of my windshield like stage scenery drawing applause for the set designer before the first actor appears. The streets were wet. In my rearview mirror, I could see my car's tread marks unrolling behind me. The quiet deepened, and when the keys dangling below the ignition shifted, causing a tinny jingling as they resettled on their ring, everything else remained undisturbed.

Nobody was out except an older man and woman on a side street. She was the abler of the two and was sweeping the street in front of their home. He was seated on a stool in the middle of the road tilting a dustbin toward her to scoop up the leaves and other debris she turned up. She more or less filled the bin and helped her husband dump it in a trash can with one motion.

As I neared the half-mile that separates downtown from the residential section, Lake Tyler was on my left and the high school on my right. The sun was already stealing the morning fog off the lake and hiding its work with an orange glare. I thought I spotted the high school's eight-man shell floating, unmanned but with all eight oars in their locks, about twenty feet offshore. I slowed down to scan the lake for the crew, or for someone embarrassed and frantic on the shore trying to rope the boat in. I saw no one on shore, and when I turned back to the lake to see if someone in the water was in trouble, I couldn't see the shell. "Precoffee hallucination," I told myself out loud. My voice sounded young.

By the time I had rounded the lake and reached downtown, I had decided that the old couple and my *Flying Dutchman* were deserving of treatment by a good novelist. Maybe the two scenes were allegorical. No, allegory doesn't sell. Maybe a novel of the macabre about the couple (What *were* they sweeping?) and a Bermuda Triangle piece about the shell. Maybe I was born to the book business. E Baker was extremely perceptive.

Chapters and Verse was one block into the business area. I hadn't thought about driving past it to get to Anson's, but there it was with window lights on and dark store behind. I had fifteen minutes to go the next block to the restaurant, so why not look in?

I don't believe in fate. Fate is mankind's greatest excuse for inexcusable behavior. I do, however, believe that there are various callings which tickle the brain and heart chemistry on certain days and lead us in new directions. The callings are always out there, but we have to be positioned just right in mood and circumstance to recognize a new melody. That morning, I was hearing a quiet but compelling symphony, and a stop at the bookstore was part of the program.

As I walked from my car to the store, I rationalized my stop with the excuse that I could sound more knowledgeable about the store when I spoke with E if I had at least peeked in. Of course E knew I'd never been in and that didn't bother her, but still I was a clothesless emperor.

I came to the first window. It featured a wooden rocking chair with an afghan draped over its front to cover the knees of an invisible person rocking. The back of the rocker had a head cushion. A small footstool with slippers casually placed on it supported the invisible reader's feet. Suspended in front of the chair, at reader's height, was an open copy of *Flynn* and stacked on a small table next to the chair were three other McDonald mysteries.

Three other "readers" were in the window, each apparently lying on his or her stomach with a book propped up in front. Their small slippers, teddy bears, and an old piece of blanket suggested these other three were children. Each was reading from a child's mystery series. The store's message board, placed in the window's corner, urged readers to "Disappear into a Mystery Series." I was impressed and later learned that such creative, no-budget windows were the pride and genius of Therese.

The doorway separated the two windows. The door itself was rectangular on its edges, but its wooden frame was crafted so that the glass insert had an irregular shape much like the tilted topknot on a soft-custard cone. Hansel and Gretel's first view of the witch's candy cottage came to mind, although I doubted the late witch had had a street number and a No Smoking decal on her door.

I passed to the second window. A leprechaun was hauling off, window right, a small cart full of books about Ireland, while a large rabbit tugged a cart full of Easter books toward the window's center from the other side. A second letter board picked up the theme with its three lines reading:

py Hap
trick's Eas
Day Holi.

A store with intelligence, humor, subtlety, and caring was going to be mine to manage; I had a life to protect.

As I realized that I was beginning to daydream, I remembered that E Baker was probably waiting for me. I looked in the front door to get a feel for the store's size and layout before I headed back to my car. Squinting to see into the darkness of Chapters and Verse, I thought I saw E Baker walking to the back down the center aisle, waving to me and smiling an "I knew you'd stop by here" smile. I smiled back at whom I thought I saw.

E was waiting for me at Anson's, sipping her coffee as I came in.

I have a friend who is a pattern finder. Her theory is that everyone acts in a consistent and progressive way that leads them to the situation they're in when she catches them and tries to analyze their life's patterns.

She tried to sort out various events and decisions in my life once to prove that my connection to a bookstore was inevitable. I'll admit she was clever.

"Did you like to collect things as a boy? Stamps? Coins? Marbles?"

"Matchbook covers."

"Aha."

"What, aha?"

"Aha, you've had a long-held desire to see assemblies of things arrayed in front of you where you can study and rearrange them."

"No, I think my late Uncle Emmett sent me a bunch of covers and got me started."

"Were you absent much from school?"

"Hardly ever. Does that mean I liked the schoolbooks?"

"Maybe. More likely, though, you liked the order in school. First period, second period, six weeks, semester. Literature, history, geography, science."

"I thought I was just unlucky enough to be pretty healthy."

"Did you decide to go up north to college to get exposure to people from other worlds?"

24

"Is Massachusetts another world?"

"No, but your choice may be clear evidence that you like a variety of experiences and viewpoints together in one place. How did you do in English?"

"Lousy."

"Who was the best English student in your high-school class?"

"David C. Miller. Unless you mean the most creative. That would have been Maitland Parks."

"Which one did you admire most?"

"The only guys I admired in high school were the guys who could make the veins in their arms stand out."

"What?"

"The guys who looked strong and adult. I admired them. Not English scholars."

"Okay. Which of the two scholars do you think of from time to time?"

"Maitland Parks. He's probably come to mind, let's see, not counting today, at least twice in the last fifteen years."

"You see. You've always sought out the creative."

On and on she went. My childhood room was papered with magazine cutouts which meant that I liked to see evidence of my reading. My first girlfriend became a commercial writer, I saved my grade-school papers, I read on the job in every job I ever held, and what else could I have become but what I was?

I think she blows about as much smoke as those folks who believe that Virgos and Cancers could eat Capricorns for lunch if the third moon were in line with the planet Mercury. A life is not a novel. It is a series of short, short stories at most. Many build on earlier stories, but only because it's too hard to change settings all the time and nobody can make frequent cast calls for new families or friends. I don't believe in the inevitability of lifetimes. Everybody picks up a pen every morning.

Ask any bookseller to categorize his customers and he'll tell you there are but two camps: those who suggest that "all your store needs is a small coffee shop or cafe in the back," and those who remain silent on the matter. The former have an intuitively good idea but poor intuition. The latter have exercised exceptional judgment at least once in their lives.

E BAKER

CHAPTER

5

In the twenties Tangelo was home to retirees, citrus growers, and people who, in one way or another, served these two groups. Fewer than four thousand people lived here when Michael Anson decided they needed a place to eat breakfast and sing.

His original sign, dated 1926, remains above the door, announcing ANSON'S: BREAKFAST, NEIGHBORS, LUNCHES. Inside, what appears to be a three-story building from the outside is arranged like a choir loft. At the lowest point, just inside the entrance, is a small area holding a checkout counter and a host's station which is a wooden music stand. The tables are placed five to a level, on four tiers which look down on this entrance area. Anson created this arrangement so that townspeople could eat breakfast, sip a second cup of coffee, and holler down at him to lead them in a song or two.

His idea caught on. Townspeople ate together here, sang, scooted their kids off to school from one of the tiers, and headed off to the bank, the groves, their yards, or wherever their day would begin. For over twenty years, Anson's place functioned as he wanted. Songs went in and out of vogue, but the new ones were probably slow to be added to the morning repertoire since people came to Anson for stability. Their day started this way, together, no matter what it brought later on. No doubt the voices were a little quieter in the Depression, but the singers were probably glad to have breakfast and company.

During the war, Anson's was often used as a meeting house by town officials concerned that Town Hall could be a target for enemy bombers. Several bass singers and tenors were saluted for the last time by their neighbors, teachers, classmates, or co-workers before they boarded the late-morning Atlantic Coast Line, heading, eventually, toward fighting and dying. Anson himself lost two sons. When the second died, so did his singing. He wanted to close his restaurant, but Maxine Paulson took it over and her family has kept it going since. Good eggs, good service, very comfortable, no music.

When I entered for my meeting with E Baker, the place was full. A friendly grandstand full of diners hovered above me, clacking dishes and discussing the Saturday beginning to unfold before them. Like countless people before me, I stood next to the music stand and scanned the voices and faces above for the party I was to meet. E waved from the center table on the highest tier.

As I headed up, I participated in another ritual fostered by Michael Anson's architecture. The steps to each tier were on alternate ends so that the top could be reached only by snaking along each lower level. It was long established that patrons would be seated at the lowest available table. In this way no one could come in without passing or being passed by everyone else inside. Everyone was seen, greeted, and, in turn, saw and greeted everyone else. Anson had a simple genius which generated thousands of smiles, comments, and kindnesses over the years.

Having nodded, waved, or mumbled for three levels to folks I knew or didn't know, I reached E. She stood up as I joined her. We sat down together at a thickly varnished oak table and began what became a three-hour breakfast.

One of Maxine Paulson's granddaughters arrived to take my order as we took our seats. E had either ordered already or, as I suspected, was always served the same breakfast. As our waitress wound her way down to the kitchen, E nodded to a man walking by our table to join his wife. After he passed, E summarized the couple.

"She's nice. Smarter than she thinks. Lately she's been reading plays. I admire anyone who can read a play, fill in all the visual things missing. He's nice, too, but he keeps his hands in his pockets when he's in the store. He's more intimidated than stubborn, I think. Good morning, Matt."

"Good morning. Do you eat here every day? They seem to know what you eat."

"Every day but Wednesday and Sunday. They're closed. I never cooked breakfast after I found out they do it better here and they wash the dishes."

That was it for the pleasantries. I was shaking my first sugar packet when E began to ask me questions about the bookstore which seemed designed to assure herself that I was what she thought I was and was worthy of managing the store. Her inquisition was far from a quiz on literary knowledge, and the intent of some of her questions isn't clear to me even now.

While most people would try to weave such questions into a less-threatening dialogue, E spilled hers out for a couple of hours without any fluff. I didn't resent this approach since it was obvious that she was concerned about herself, me, and the store. She was clearly rooting for me and listened carefully to my answers.

We're forbidden by social convention from asking directly most of the things we'd most like to know: "Rachel, if your husband died and my wife left, would you think of me?" "Why do you want me to laugh all the time?" "James, why do I see the same sadness in your eyes that I feel must be in mine?" I would summarize E's unaskable questions as, "So. You've lived for a little while. What are you? Can you be trusted with something which is part of the fabric of this town? Can you ask such questions yourself? Can you hear the answers? Do we have in common the few things which are most important to me?"

The questions E asked out loud stayed within the rules. Many seemed to be standard interview questions, though it was understood that standard answers wouldn't do. Others seemed to come from that other agenda I couldn't second-guess. I enjoyed answering each one and looked forward to the next, probably because most presented an opportunity for self-flattery.

Although there might have been thirty or so, I can remember only a few. Some of my answers didn't please me at the time but, as the breakfast progressed, I realized that E was satisfied. That morning, and from time to time since then, I found myself smiling, relieved and full of pride that I had passed a test few people prepare for or allow themselves to take. Fewer still are lucky enough to have someone who cares enough to administer such a test.

I've improved some of my answers over time. Others, I'm ashamed to say, were a bit too optimistic in light of my laziness or lack of attention.

29

"What did you think when I asked you to manage the store out of the blue?" she began.

"That you wanted me to manage the store. That is, it seemed natural at the time. It seemed we were communicating on an unusual level. I haven't questioned wanting to do it since you asked. I am more than curious as to why you selected me, though. We'd never met."

"I didn't conduct any research about you, to tell the truth. My instincts have always been good on the most important matters. Are you worried about what the rest of the staff will think when you parachute in?"

"Not really worried since I don't know them. I doubt they'd expect you to behave in the normal way when it comes to running the store or hiring a manager."

" 'Please, God, don't let me be normal.' Some people pay their bills only when they have to. What about you?"

"Get a bill, pay a bill. 'Plant a radish, get a radish.' "

"What would you do if the man with the adult bookstore in the county wanted to open one downtown, and you were asked to appear before the town council to give your opinion?"

"I'd hate to have to appear and would tell them that. Then I'd have to tell them that the guy's taste is in the gutter as far as I am concerned but I can't condone censoring what he can sell, since I don't think we know how to draw the line on what's okay and what's not. I would never want to show book burners where the matches are."

"What kind of books would you stay away from?"

"What doesn't sell, I hope. Also anything that I think is trash. If it's my choice, then I'd say it's okay to write most anything not libelous, but I don't have to sell it. The politics of a book don't bother me much unless there's too much hate. I think I'd order anything for anybody, though. I may not stock much by Richard Nixon."

"Are there people in town you don't like?"

"Of course."

"If a customer were about to buy a book you've read and know to be a lemon, would you say something?"

"No."

"If a customer liked a certain type of book and a new one came in that she'd like, would you say something?"

30

"I'd probably drop her a card if we had a system for that, or just tell her when she came in. Of course it might be more fun to let her find it herself when she came in not knowing we had it."

"How will you know if running Chapters and Verse was a good decision on your part?"

"By what I overhear about the store from our customers. Maybe by how the town looks when I drive home in the evening."

"Do you think people here are better book people than people in other places?"

"I've never thought about people as book people except in college, where book was a verb. People here like it here. They care about local history, their family's development, the small changes. That means contemplation and quality are important to them, and maybe then books could be especially important."

I finished my breakfast during this exchange, but E hadn't begun hers except to sip some coffee. Only after she had stopped questioning me and we paused for a silent minute or two, would she eat. She didn't seem the type to eat pigs in a blueberry blanket, but that's what she had ordered. Maxine's granddaughter must have been keeping an eye on her during the questioning because when E picked up a fork to eat, her cold breakfast was neatly replaced by an identical hot one.

We didn't talk much while she ate. Both of us were reviewing the test results. My confidence was running high, but the main mystery of the morning remained unresolved. I felt it was time to put the mike in front of my new employer.

"What's the truth you didn't tell me?" I asked in my version of the calm tone she had used when putting me through my paces. E looked up for a moment, then finished the last two bites of her pancake. Then she did something no one does at restaurants but which makes perfect sense. She stood up, stretched to let her meal slide down a bit, and sat back down. I started to chuckle. E smiled at me and began a laugh herself. "You're certainly a cheap laugh," she said.

"I'm laughing at the idea of everyone who eats at a restaurant standing up at least once during a meal and sitting back down. Restaurants will all look like jack-in-the-box assembly lines. Then the table-etiquette books will have to be changed, and distances between tables increased, chair casters will become more popular . . ."

"I'm giving you Chapters and Verse."

By now non sequiturs were the rule in our conversations, but this one was a stunner. Stalling my reaction with clumsy humor, I stood up. I looked down at E Baker, studied a purple-and-yellow feather in her navy felt hat, and asked on the way down, "How?"

"Don't you mean 'Why'?"

"No. I know you'll have a why I can't argue with, so let's start with how."

"Actually I'm selling you the store because my lawyer says I can't give it to you and because I'll need some money. It was her idea, not mine. I would have been pleased to give it to you and let you send me some money from it every once in a while if I get caught short. Lawyers don't think any transaction made from the heart will stand up in court and every transaction could go to court. That philosophy reminds me of the comic strip in which a man is the only attorney in the county and still making no money. His fortune is made when a second attorney moves in. Anyway you'll have to pay up, but we'll work out whatever terms you need."

When money comes into a conversation, most of us drop down a template of caution to assess things. Little ugly voices call out hard words like motive, trade-off, risk, and fairness. Lessons of the years—"protect yourself" and "look down the road"—are applied grimly but without question. Our faces tighten a bit and our thoughts are inevitably of ourselves and the papers and numbers with which we've been taught to measure the success of our activities.

Maybe I should have been thinking about E's terms. Maybe I should have questioned, even for a moment, the idea of buying a business I'd never even seen from the inside. Instead I was daydreaming. I'd wear long-sleeved white shirts, cuffs folded back, and jeans—no tie. I'd take over humbly, dedicated, working long hours to learn, learn, learn. "No," I'd say, "I'm not E Baker. You knew her. No one could be like her. I'm just trying to build my ideas onto hers." I'd take a while to put my own brand on the store. What was my brand?

Like two children dividing up a pillowcase full of trick-or-treat candy, E Baker and I negotiated the sale of Chapters and Verse. There was no question that we would each do well in the negotiation and, in my case at least, the issue of whether the treats had been earned was overlooked. In a matter of minutes, I learned that the store showed a modest after-tax profit each year, and that E took a modest salary. She learned how much I could give her from my inheritance to start, and we agreed that I'd send her seven hundred dollars a month for the next ten years and increase that with inflation so she could be comfortable. This was not a hostile takeover. The maneuvers lasted less time than our next cup of coffee.

I wanted to talk about the store. Who did the buying? How did they keep up with what sold? How would I be trained? How long would E stay around to help me? Questions lined up in my mind, and as I posed each one to E, I started to understand how little I knew about the running of my new enterprise.

She answered everything with facts. The lease was for fifteen more years. The staff divided up the ordering by publisher and interest. Wholesalers provided over 60 percent of the stock. They needed an inventory system. Sales rose a steady 4 to 6 percent a year. Credit-card companies took a percentage but you had to have them. Gift wrapping, book mailing, out-of-print searches, yes. Encyclopedia sales, no. Windows, Therese—she knew what to do. Receiving, shared. I should do some also. Advertising, worthless. Magazines—low discount, mostly a nuisance. Evan ordered them. Publishers' representatives—she had a list of the ones with the best advice. Others were to be tolerated and ignored.

The more I learned, the less I felt I knew. Then E told me that she did not wish to stay after I took over. I felt as if I'd been given a baton, a skilled, well-rehearsed orchestra, and a score I'd never seen and was about to be kicked out onstage before a sophisticated audience. The honor was great, the disaster potential high. I asked her to stay for six months to teach me about the store, but she would agree to stay for only two. That's when we moved our breakfast talk into a discussion of why E wanted to sell.

At the time I felt that E was explaining quite thoroughly why she wanted to leave Chapters and Verse behind. Trying to recall her explanation, though, I find that I'm left only with a few facts and without any sense of the feelings that had made her want to leave. Maybe E herself hadn't analyzed her feelings, and that's why I can't remember them. More likely she simply didn't tell me any more than she wanted to, preferring to keep her complicated impulses to herself.

E told me she was going to travel, take photographs, and compile a book on teachers. Her itinerary was already set with twenty-three stops in small cities in the southern U.S. from Florida to Texas. She said she had a nibble from a publisher, a desire to travel, and an interest in photography that had been building over the years. Her black-and-whites would capture parents teaching children how to hold a bat, children in strollers explaining secrets of animals to their parents, and young professors teaching classes of older people. The world was full of teachers trying to share lessons of all sorts. Of course E knew that such books don't sell well, but she predicted that I would also come to a point when I'd have to find some way to put a book on the shelves with whatever talents I could muster.

"Every day those innocents on the shelf will work on you," she said. "You won't notice it for a while, perhaps, but they'll be goading you. 'What can you do?' they'll want to know. Sooner or later, you'll try to answer."

I didn't agree with her on that one, and I told her of the unsuccessful book I'd started and my own photographs. She became quite interested in my technique and my intentions. E seemed amazed and sad that I had thrown out my work in frustration when things hadn't worked out. In fact the last part of our breakfast was spent discussing my nearly forgotten literary efforts and E's feelings on preserving old creations and keeping doors open. Nothing else was said of Chapters and Verse.

As we wound our way down from the top perch at Anson's, I was excited and apprehensive. E, as always, seemed satisfied that she was doing what she should. She left me at the door with a handshake and a smiling "You'll be hearing from my lawyer." I didn't see her again until I showed up for work. Two months after that, she was gone.

As I drove home from Anson's, through downtown, past the lake, and through the streets that had been bright and still earlier, I began to realize that I would be taking my place in the history and lives of others. Like the family doctor, the town's mayor, the coach or the pharmacist, I was going to be a childhood memory, part of "this is what the world is made of." For the first time, I wondered how I'd be remembered.

> *The customer is always right, even when you both*
> *know he's wrong, except that he loses his privilege to*
> *be right when he gets too loud; in that case he is right*
> *at the time but never again.*
>
> E BAKER

CHAPTER

6

E held the phone to her ear. Her eyebrows rose and she looked at me as she spoke to the caller. "No, sir. Books with price stickers from other bookstores were not purchased at Chapters and Verse and may not be returned here." She paused to listen. She frowned. "No, we never use their stickers. That's okay. Next time, come in here to buy and I'll show you which ones might work best for you."

That was how I learned of a particular return policy. E taught me to run Chapters and Verse one episode at a time. All I had to do was watch and listen. Soon enough, everything I'd need to know would come up and she'd have to deal with it. Bills would come in, packing slips would be missing, a customer would need a book no longer in print. Paperbacks would be shipped with the hardbacks still on the shelf, a front window light would go out, or somebody would call in sick. All that was easy to pick up. The real lesson in all of it was that there is this rhythm, an irresistible, undeniable rhythm in here—a steady, crazy spin from this subject to that, this request to that one.

For two months I watched and listened as E scurried about her constantly changing domain. She was capable of a gearshift a minute, and the work demanded something like that. She played with the changes; she reveled in them.

E was fast, faster than the rest of us by far. She would scan the cart full of books to shelve, scoop up a bunch, and place them on their respective shelves without stopping to question what went where or which books to put away first. The rest of

35

us might take three times as long to do the same job. We'd anguish over the correct section for *The Philosophy of the Left Hander* or *The Tao of Pooh*, but she wouldn't. E Baker was like those showman waiters at the Japanese steak houses who slice and trim and serve various meats and vegetables with the lightning flick of their wrists and flash of their sharp knives. Those guys all have Band-Aids on their fingers, but E never complained about so much as a paper cut.

Once, when she caught me marveling at her ease in shelving books in the right place, she told me, "If you don't know where to shelve a book, put it in Social Sciences. You can always make a case for Social Sciences."

If an invoice came in wrong or a publisher called for payment on something already paid, she would scowl. "Publishers' bookkeeping departments are repositories for the incompetent. They should all turn themselves in and be done with it." She would straighten out that particular confusion and move on. When a truck shipment of books arrived and she needed receiving help in the back, she'd call to us that "Emily Brontë and Allen Ginsberg just drove in. Help!"

Her real genius was with the customers. These she served in a style only E Baker could get away with. Never would I be able to tell the mayor, "Now Andrew, you read this book. You better finish it before your trip to Atlanta, too, because if you're in the middle, you won't want to go. If you don't go, we might not get that road money you promised, so take this home now and start on it tonight."

She was gruff and she was honest about her opinions. "I never liked Dreiser. He may be a standard, but he reads like a colorless reporter," or, "Tom Robbins held something back in . . . *Woodpecker*. It's good, but . . . *Cowgirls*—now a big piece of his heart is in there." Sometimes a customer would disagree and she loved that. Her mind might be changed on a matter of opinion, but it took someone with courage to try to do it. Her undeniable goodwill was all that kept her from being intimidating.

One morning, while I was working the counter with E, a child met his father at the front of the store. For the first time, the boy inquired about his father's selections. The father was stunned; he was at once facing a mature son and his own father. His instinct was to sluff off the question but he knew he

36

shouldn't. He handed over his small stack to be reviewed, swapping them for his son's:

> an offbeat novel about a Southern adolescent
>
> a book of E. B. White essays
>
> a picture book of small-town Iowa
>
> for
>
> an introduction to the planets
>
> book four of a detective series
>
> a biography of John Adams, the second president

It was surely one of the great trades of our time. E remained silent, smiling, satisfied.

When they left, as E was showing me how to change the tape on the cash register, she said, "There are people on the shelves, people in the store. After a while you can't tell the books from the people, the people from the books. They take turns and it's all nicely confusing when you find they have switched again."

That's the way she taught me.

Most people turn right when they enter stores. I learned that from a store-planning book which I read before I came to work at Chapters and Verse because I wanted to show E that I wasn't a complete novice at retailing.

I proudly shared that highly technical bit of knowledge with E about a week after I came to work. I proposed that we change the store layout to take advantage of my discovery. E raised her eyebrows, looked toward the front of the store, and suggested some research was in order. Then she left the project to me.

I focused my attention on the stacked risers we had dead center when you walked in the front door. New arrivals had always been placed there. I picked a busy Saturday to check the behavior ("traffic pattern," the book would have called it) of ten customers chosen at random to see if they went left or right when they came to the riser.

I remembered my college statistics course, in which a Professor Hand had seemed to make a religion of true randomness. I remembered also that Professor Hand had inadvertently driven his point home by being killed in a one-in-a-million accident. He was

37

leaning out of the campus clock tower to call to a colleague below when a cable snapped in the clock and he was minute-handed to his death. Eternally impressed by his instruction, I didn't want to skew my observations to favor early risers or late shoppers, so I selected the first two customers each hour for five hours. I think I liked the idea that my research took a full five hours since I was looking for an exhaustive study.

My research verified the right-turn theory. Six people turned right as smartly and predictably as the tuba section in the marching band that struts to a yard line and peels off to an assigned yard mark to help make the O in GATORS. Another customer stopped just inside the store, paused for some time to peruse the terrain, and finally chose the road most traveled. The theory seemed sound.

There were three other subjects, however. One, an angered husband, watched his wife head right, and then he stomped off to the left. I was going to toss him out of my sample, but I heard Professor Hand, still groggy from his blow to the head, scolding me about tampering with randomness: "Statistically one of every ten husbands may be mad at his wife. Mad husbands may always turn left, but that's another hypothesis. Who are you to violate a perfect sample? Sit down." I sat down.

I did toss one person out of the study. This was a woman who came in, closed the door behind her, pressed her nose against the door glass, looked out at her embarrassed teenage daughter on the sidewalk and yelled, "There! Am I a fun person now?" I eliminated her as a subject since she didn't turn either right or left.

Two people in my survey turned left with the same certainty and lack of provocation as those who turned right. One of these, an out-of-towner, made the biggest purchase of the day. He hauled a stack of hardback biographies to the counter. They were serious works about British playwrights and essayists, and his purchase enhanced both our daily take and our quiet pride as a source of serious literary materials. The perfect customer, he was. The other left turner bought an eighty-dollar book on Monet.

For a while these two customers made me struggle. Most people, seven of ten in my sample, go right. Big buyers go left. Had I explained why most businesses go belly-up? What does a store planner do? Fake right and go left? Make everyone go left? Set up a cattle chute so everyone stays center? No. Choices are the essence of a good bookstore, I reasoned, so the decision was not where to direct customers, but what to put in the path of their choice.

E had already made this discovery, of course. She had developed what I call the haunted-house approach. As the customer bobs along this way or that, more or less suspecting a surprise, we place assorted witches and ghosts for him to discover. We stick books we like best, or, I admit, books we'd really like to retire from the shelves, on the ends of gondolas.

When a customer rounds a corner, he'll be startled by a European atlas he can't believe we carry. At another turn two friends will discover together the entire Tom Swift series (not Tom Swift, Jr., but the real Tom): "I can't believe they still print these. I loved them when I was about eleven." Everything written by or about Anäis Nin will jump out at an unsuspecting store traveler as she turns her back on Biography. Even the most seasoned book shopper can be surprised by a beautifully bound re-release of an old Andre Norton title. It's so easy to make people happy here.

It was late in the day on a Thursday. The sun was bright but falling, and our front windows had turned to that afternoon orange which takes over from the fluorescent light inside.

E was holding two novels by the same author. One, written under a pen name, was a spy thriller which sold well. The second was in our literature section and was a beautifully written, slow-selling contemporary novel. E was shaking her head. She spoke quietly and slowly.

"Sometimes I can feel those passages which contain the author's heart. I usually find these in 'lesser' works. Matthew, sometimes I can hear authors like this one, maybe a thirty-two-year-old schoolteacher from Vermont, who has decided that he can quit teaching high-school shop if he publishes just one more book. I can picture him meeting with his agent. He's just completed a work on a farm family which endures the tedium of Vermont winters and the loss of a daughter, and which has discovered the poetry in daily survival. His soul is in the book, and it's as close as he feels he can come to the novel he's always wanted to write.

"Unfortunately the book comes on the heels of his best-seller about a couple of sisters who are harassed by mysterious red beams and beeping noises which seem to follow them when they play canasta. The beams and beeps are revealed as mistakes made by high-tech types in the CIA, and the book has sold well in both hard and softcover.

"The agent is one of those whose main interest is in books he can sell to the movies. He flops the manuscript of the new novel on the table in the uptown restaurant to which he's taken the young author—the agent's 'hot property.' A water ring from the agent's citrus-and-alcohol drink makes its way into the bottom pages of the manuscript, and the author fights the urge to grab the papers. 'Maybe the agent has a second copy. Maybe ten are circulating now,' he thinks. 'Agents are somewhat uncaring sometimes, but they are necessary. They do see value,' he assures himself.

"Then the agent asks if the author has begun work on another, more saleable novel. 'Real writing is okay, but have you thought about a book on lasers which penetrate the ozone and rip thin tunnels completely through the earth? How about letting the two sisters return in a sequel and turn the tables on the CIA? Of course you have your own ideas . . .'

"The agent reaches for a pen to write down these two terrific story lines. He spills his drink on the author's new novel."

I learned that among her other talents, E Baker could tell a decent story. However I couldn't let her become soft, even for a moment.

"E," I said, "we both know that the agent is right and the writer is sincere. No one will make a living off books about that family."

"Just so we keep a few places on the shelves for these special goods," she said.

Some people are more chapter than verse. Some are all chapter, and some all verse.

E BAKER

CHAPTER

7

I work the front on Saturdays as E always did. The front is a nine-foot stretch of checkout counter just re-covered in a Formica pattern called Royal Oak. The back lip of the counter is spotted with assorted taped labels, like "Lawrence's slips," "Police 446-2444, Grimes," *or* "NO CHECKS FROM MR. J. THOMPSON (his wife says) or SUSAN DESTIN—NYC." *Down below, we keep books people have special ordered and our bags, mailing envelopes, scissors, and the like.*

On slow Saturdays the things behind the counter become quite important to those of us stationed there. It's easy to pass time speculating on why Mrs. Tibbs ordered two copies of Chinese Watercolors, *or why three people, unrelated as far as we know, ordered Wicker's book on Attica. I've been known to redesign our bag logo two or three times an hour on midsummer Saturdays.*

Lawrence, when he shares counter duties with me, particularly enjoys developing theories on the items people leave in our store. He has several ideas about why sunglasses are left behind more than most things. Typical of these theories is the idea that their wearers are subconsciously resisting any attempt to put life in darkness and thereby are fighting with the evil side of their psyches. The most plausible of his theories is that T-shirts usually don't have pockets.

The counter is one of those special places in the world, created by man and the accidents of society, which statistically valid samples of humankind will visit at semi-regular intervals. Manning this station on Saturdays means that I see a rotation of people and activity through a stroboscope: I know what goes on here, what the regulars read from week to week, but virtually nothing of what goes on when these same people aren't in view.

I call my regular Saturday customers Weekly Readers. The real Weekly Reader was a newsprint magazine we used to receive each Thursday in elementary school in the fifties. It told us about landmark balloon trips, historic political meetings, advance-design automobiles, and the establishment of assorted countries. If it had a political point of view, it was not apparent to us in the fifth grade; if it was supposed to generate controversy, it failed. We just accepted it as part of school life and as the source for find-a-word puzzles or current-events tests. Despite its lack of excitement, I looked forward to the little newspaper. It was a voice from outside somewhere. Our teacher didn't write it and it was more a part of current life than our ancient textbooks.

For most of my Weekly Readers, I've concocted a non-bookstore life based on gross extrapolations from their behavior in the store. I've decided Reggie Patterson practices law quietly, treats his family as he imagines the family patriarch should, and probably wishes he could disappear to Costa Rica to grow macadamias and sit on his plantation house porch overlooking the Pacific. Ruth Ellen Boatwright weaves. She lives in a rented "caretaker's cottage" behind her landlord's house, and has a cat named Bessie and a boyfriend in Indiana she hasn't seen for six years. Stan Masters attends every high-school sporting event and writes summaries of them for a personal scrapbook. Milton Bates does whatever his second wife tells him to do.

For some people I create lives I wish they would live. I wish that Margery Dawson would sneak out on occasional evenings to walk alone through the woods behind her house composing music for the trees. I wish Robert Helmsly would be called by his banker "with some terrible news" just once so he could spend an evening without smugness. I wish Melinda Tallgrass would get her few minutes in the limelight soon.

My regulars, just by showing up every Saturday, are taking on more and more importance for me. Since we're together every week, we're measuring our days together, growing older together, watching books come and go together.

A couple of weeks after I'd come to Chapters and Verse, E took me to the Windsor. It was a Thursday evening and she had called me at home, again operating under the assumption that my own schedule would fit hers. "It's my night at the Windsor. You should be there so I can show you around."

We hadn't spoken about the hotel before and I was surprised at this hint that part of my new responsibilities might include it. As far as I knew, the hotel had no bookshop of its own and E kept no office there.

The only other time I'd been to the Windsor was when I was eighteen. I was trying to hook up with the right college and had written to about twenty of them as a project in typing class. Probably because Tangelo is between the fertile college recruiting grounds of Atlanta and Miami, a representative from Dartmouth stopped in town for the night to interview me. Maybe he stopped because my letter to Dartmouth and the others included a slightly misleading reference to my out-of-school work with a nearby atomic-research organization. Nuclear power was a good thing in those days since it didn't exist yet. Anyone who purported to be part of the great effort to tame the atom got some attention.

I remember sitting in the lobby and talking with a Mr. Teague who seemed confident and mature to me at the time, but who was perhaps all of twenty-three. He joked about the hotel stationery which included no street address in its letterhead. I tried to explain that we had just the four postmen and so we kept things simple in Tangelo. We talked for a while about Dartmouth and about me. Soon enough, Mr. Teague learned that my experience with research into the atom was limited to three afternoons when I had filled in for Joey Braverson who was on vacation from his filing job. Since I probably wasn't a future Nobel Prize winner in atomic physics, Mr. Teague turned the conversation to how long it took for the newest movies to show up in town.

I didn't bother to apply to his school, but I remembered the inside of the Windsor because it smelled like wood, leather, and history.

E and I met in the rear parking lot. "You don't know anyone like William Casten" was how she greeted me.

"It's eight thirty," I said. "I don't even know William Casten, and he has not invited me to meet him."

E laughed. "He will know how to make you feel welcome. He knows you're coming over sometime, so I decided tonight would be the time."

I enjoyed pushing at the quiet weight of the hotel's rear door, with its neatly lettered WINDSOR POINT HOTEL painted in rich black enamel on well-polished wood. A small brass light fixture was over the door for the sole purpose of illuminating these letters. Attention to detail was obviously important, very important, at the Windsor.

Later I learned that William Casten, who owned the Windsor, noticed the smallest things, often overlooking the more obvious, and knew at once when something had been moved or left unattended. The finicky and relentlessly old-fashioned maintenance of even its back door made his hotel comfortable and predictable, like the home of a favorite aunt.

We walked through a short, carpeted corridor from the hotel's rear to the front. On the left were the two elevators. The dials above them showed one to be on the lobby level and the other on the hotel's top floor, number three. Both cars were awaiting instruction. On the right were rooms 100, 102, and William Casten's office. There was a dim light in the milk glass of his door which made his office seem to glow. I could hear him humming inside.

"He's working on his musical," E said quietly as we passed his office and headed through the swinging doors at the end of the hall.

The lobby was a silent night stage. It was the proverbial drawing-room comedy set with its bookcases, leather chairs, oriental rug, and writing tables holding banker's lamps. The table where I'd chatted with Mr. Teague about Dartmouth was exactly where it had been that night. The closed doors to the hall, the ones we'd just passed through, awaited entrances of various players.

The wall behind the tables was filled with bookshelves. I'm sure E was waiting for me to notice them. Like bookcases in hotels, inns, ships' libraries, and other public places, these held books for exchange. The rule for such bookcases is unwritten and universal. It is so well understood that I doubt it has ever been spoken aloud: Guests may borrow or bestow at will.

I believe that very few borrow from these shelves without leaving a substitute or returning the book borrowed. Since many people travel with books they plan to leave behind, the stock on such shelves is always on the increase. I can't think of another public sharing of possessions which works in this wonderful way.

44

E caught me staring at them. "These are one of very few remaining evidences of the nobility of civilization in the country," she said. She took a few moments to look over each of the shelves. "There are another four or five years of shelf space left before there will be a need to cull. We don't have to remove a book now unless it is frayed to the point of sadness."

"Okay. Why are we here?" I loved to play this game with her.

"We're here because I've kept these shelves in order for William Casten for seven years and that responsibility now passes to you."

"Relationship to Chapters and Verse?"

"None."

"And?"

"And so I do it, and you will, because there are books to be tended and because one of the world's finest men appreciates and deserves such a service."

"How often do we 'tend' this stock and what is it we do?" I deliberately avoided asking about William Casten and why he merited such praise from E. She would answer, or he would, at some time I knew I could not influence.

"Weekly works nicely and alphabetical by author is good enough."

By now I know that weekly does work nicely and alphabetical by author is good enough. Each Thursday night, I park in the back lot, walk through the hall, through those swinging doors, and scan the shelves. I may notice that the Helen MacInnes books have been purged completely, and I'll assume that some guest, probably one of the salesmen, was an insomniac mystery addict. The fat best-seller which was left last week, a hardback Sidney Sheldon, is also gone. I could have predicted that. There are three new children's books—no mystery there, as I remember selling them to a family a few days ago after they'd spent too artificial a day at one of the tourist parks.

The challenge in the bookcases is not to place the books in their proper order; the skill is in spotting new books and trying to match them with donors. I usually try to do this with Stephen, the evening desk clerk. At eight thirty, which is usually when I come in, Stephen is behind the front desk, stacking up his papers and preparing to leave for the night. He goes home to study. Stephen has been working his way through graduate school by working the evening shift. He goes to classes by day, works at the front desk from late afternoon until nine, and then goes home to study art history. He's been after his degree for six years and I admire his tenacity. At twenty-four, Stephen has somehow escaped the disturbing and sad fate of others his age who have been convinced that they are worth huge salaries because they know how to spend their money. I don't know who has told them that.

Stephen knows I will hold up a book and ask him who left it. He can't be sure of the donor, of course, since most books are left in the rooms or at the desk after morning checkout when he doesn't work. Still he patiently watches me wave a Frank Herbert or an Ian Fleming and takes his best guess as to who left it for me to alphabetize.

I don't know if the people he describes ever stayed in the hotel. Perhaps a French diplomat did indeed leave the two-volume dictionary because he gave up trying to learn English to impress Janice Cochran at the bank. Perhaps there was a secretive woman carrying a viola case who swapped *Candide* for *The Woman's Room* and left the hotel housekeeper a fifty-dollar tip. Stephen says that's what happened and he does fit these real or imagined guests to the new books very nicely.

That first night at the hotel, William Casten himself appeared at the front desk. I saw him emerge from the back hall—a short, thin, dapper man with white hair and eyebrows. I guessed that he was in his midseventies. He wore a three-piece suit and walked with a youthful bounce in his step. His eyes passed back and forth over the lobby as he approached us.

William Casten was, of course, the reason the Windsor was a bit of polished rail in an otherwise indifferent downtown. He cared about the hotel he had operated since the fifties. He insisted that all guests sign in, and that they be greeted by their proper names as they were welcomed at the registration desk. He insisted that the glass over the pictures in the lobby be cleaned twice a day. William Casten cared a great deal about presentation and the pleasant surprise caused by a special touch here and there. To him these were matters of honor.

He started speaking as he came through the doors, never raising his voice so that he was easily heard only when he made it to where we were by the front desk. "We've got twelve singles going," his discourse began at the doors, "all of them dead tired

46

and probably asleep—salesmen. There's a party of some college kids in 308, but they're not getting along so well judging by the way they didn't say anything to each other when they checked in. Right, Stephen? There are three families on two. They stopped asking for cots and towels about ten. I do like nights like this one. It's the diversity."

He continued on with his monologue for a few minutes, mostly talking about a letter he'd received from his brother, Reuben, who was retiring from his printing business in Memphis. After a while he stopped for a moment to introduce himself to me.

"Welcome to the Windsor, Matthew Mason. E has told me that you've been working with her. I see that she's also told you about our little project here. No obligations of any kind, of course, but it would be wonderful to have you come by every week or so. Let me know when and I'll have coffee with you. If I'm humming or singing in my office, please don't knock. I'll know you're here and be out soon enough. Do you like musicals?"

"If they don't mention Broadway in any song, or feature dancing fruit, and if the chorus is busy when the principals are singing."

"Good enough, no idle chorus members. Welcome again to the Windsor."

Then William slapped a stack of papers down on the registration counter. He stared at this stack which he'd brought along from his office. E, Stephen, and I stared at it also. We had no choice but to be captured by whatever captured William Casten.

When he'd secured our full attention in this way, he announced that he'd finally developed a title for his musical. "I will call it *Savory Characters*," he said. He paused to let his announcement sink in. Just saying these words seemed to lift him a few inches off the ground. I watched E as she watched this wonderfully energetic man. She smiled in a way I've never seen her smile for anyone else. William Casten had clearly earned a special place in her mysterious heart.

"That's the title of the big song in the third act. I see the female lead, that's LeeAnn—remember E?—stopping the show with that one. I want to save the title song for the end. The audience always wants to know the why of the title, of course, and I can see them nodding their now-I-see's while LeeAnn belts out 'Savory Characters' and the policemen's chorus backs her up. What do you think, E?"

The answer didn't matter. E told me later that he'd been struggling with a title since she could remember there being a Windsor, and he had mentioned his musical during every conversation they'd had. She also admitted that she had no real sense of what the play was about, since William's various descriptions of it included scenes ranging from a bungled bank robbery to a campfire sing after a calf-branding session. Each of the scenes, she said, was beautiful and complete in itself, but she couldn't discern any link between them.

None of that bothered E. What she loved was the joy inside this man. He, alone, could make her laugh at will and place her happily in an audience. "There are two kinds of people in the world," she told me that night as we were getting into our cars in the Windsor's parking lot, "those who are alive and everyone else. William Casten is alive."

I learned that for myself later on when E began to travel and I spent some time with William.

*Are the people who write these books the ones who go
in that back room?*

YOUNG CUSTOMER

CHAPTER

8

*Many of our regulars and most of our staff
think about writing their own books. It's hard not
to believe that you can write books better than
some you read. Some customers, like Molly
Tenbie, actually produce a decent work and get it
published. We did quite well with Molly's*
Children. *Some others probably learn early that time, craft, and
sustained interest aren't available to everyone. Still others write
poetry or autobiography which might appeal only to selected and
tolerant members of their nuclear family. Some self-publish their
works and proudly troop them in to take their place in our growing
local-authors' section. A three-month time limit on shelf space is
about all that keeps the books in the section rotating. We do much
better with our magazines and books on how to be a writer than we
do with the works by their local readers.*

*It didn't take me long before I succumbed to the dangerous logic
that if a book I was reading seemed poorly written, I must be able to
write a better one. I deserved a place on the shelves as much as the
next guy.*

*Shortly after I bought the store, I realized that I had also bought
a largely undeserved reputation as a man of letters. Anyone who
"knew" all those books and authors must be an exceptionally well-
read cultural filter at the least, and a critic or secret author at best. I
forgot that I knew most books by cover, price, and publisher rather
than content; my literary perch was easy to accept. Man can adapt
quickly to just about any type of flattery.*

*Armed with my instant reputation and my regular dismay at
some of the work that found its way to our shelves, I decided to take
my turn. I already had an idea for a book which had taken root*

49

when I was a child watching "The Naked City." There were eight million stories in that city, I had been told after Paul Burke had solved a murder or robbery. I was only eight or nine years old at the time, but I bought into the one-person, one-story idea for life.

My idea was simple and, I thought, revolutionary (read "marketable") in that I was sure it would make people appreciate each other as never before. I would identify twenty strangers, all common people, have them reveal their stories to me, and record my findings. Twenty strangers times ten pages equals a two-hundred-page sleeper destined for the Times best-seller list. I began picking out a suit for the talk-show circuit even before I bought a legal pad for my first interview. Should I have a book signing for myself at the store? Would that seem immodest? No, my readers would insist that I do. This writing business was easy.

I prepared a query letter, stressing the notion of finding the miracle or hidden life in everyone, and sent it out. After seven politely written form letters rejecting my concept for "our list," one kind reader penciled in a note below the form letter daring me to find one such story and get it published by a magazine. "People just aren't that interesting and those that are won't open up. There's a reason why common people are common people. Most are modest for good reason." I didn't scare. I would find my silent heroes and write their stories.

The nearest Naked City to me was Orlando—a city growing so fast that most of its residents are newcomers. Many people there at any one time are tourists. More and more people are flocking there for the opportunities to make money from each other. Careers and entrepreneurship appear to be the gods, along with fun, fun, fun. In short, if there were ever a population which threatened to be shallow, self-serving, and boring, this was it. My theory, of course, was that these folks in the booming city of strip shopping centers and fake rocks were no different from the colorful characters supposedly rocking on every small-town porch. My faith in human nature was at stake.

Downtown Orlando was prospering like the rest of the area. The familiar cycle of boom, exodus, decay, and rebuilding had already taken place except that the last phase, which takes most cities decades and which many cities have not yet begun, had only taken about five years in Orlando. Cranes and high rises were added to the skyline as quickly as financing could be arranged.

Orange Avenue at Central is the heart of downtown. Address numbers start there. It was once the intersection of department stores and dress shops. People came regularly to downtown (the women

50

wearing white gloves), and to that intersection, to shop in such numbers that a special catty-corner pedestrian crossing time was allowed.

Now the corner hosts two bank high rises, one lawyer high rise, and a government office building. Men and women in suits have hooked themselves to briefcases and replaced those families with their shopping bags as the pedestrian populace. Each of these men or women, and his or her briefcase, is assigned to an office in one of the high rises. They have jobs to do, usually in a large company, usually with some title. According to local television, they spend their free time water skiing, boating, partying by convenient pools, or visiting franchised bar/restaurants meeting like-minded fun seekers. How could these people have stories to tell? I knew they would surprise everyone, and so I settled on the people in the four downtown buildings for my twenty stories.

Each Wednesday, I set aside three hours to drive to Orlando to conduct my interviews. With two sessions per "subject" and another week to write up each chapter, I would have my discoveries ready for print in a little over a year. During that time I could secure a publisher who appreciated the undeniable importance of my work, and I could tell anyone who asked that I was working on a book.

On my first Wednesday, I walked into a bank lobby ready to talk to my first fascinating subject. I hadn't planned well. Other than tellers, who obviously couldn't take the time to tell me about their secret lives as underwater photographers or teachers of immigrant children, the only human I could talk to was a receptionist who was not free to talk for more than a minute or two without responding to a telephone call. I asked for a list of bank officers and phone numbers and decided to call one from the lobby phone.

"Fay Lane Parker, Security Officer" jumped at me from the list. Was she a police officer, did she sell certain financial "securities," or was she there to give customers a sense of security as they handed over the results of years of working to this metal-and-glass building? I called her at 2237.

Her phone was so close to me that I could hear it ring when I called. Fay Lane Parker was the keeper of the keys to the safety-deposit boxes and drawers which were housed in a spotless vault just off the main lobby. Fay Lane was going to lunch in the bank cafeteria in twenty minutes and invited me along, if I was willing to eat "food prepared by cooks who had almost learned to cook in the army." That seemed a fair price to pay for an interview.

In the course of lunch, I realized that I had hit the jackpot my first time out. Fay Lane Parker had come to the bank directly from the slammer. She was, in fact, a parolee whom the bank had hired as part of a "Help Them Out" program sponsored by the bank president's husband.

Fay Lane had shot her stepbrother's best friend who had taken to visiting her, without warning or welcome, via her bedroom window. After three such visits and screaming the best friend away, she had pleaded with her stepbrother to call him off. The stepbrother allowed as how he, too, was afraid of his friend, but let Fay Lane borrow his .38 to discourage continued visits. On the next intrusion, Fay Lane pumped three of the gun's four bullets into the wall, but the fourth she managed to direct into her visitor's ankle. He went down, screaming for his lawyer.

Fay Lane was charged and convicted on a malicious wounding count, served ten months in state prison, during which time she helped found "Help Them Out" from within, and even I could turn her story into a good one. I wrote it up, labeled it "Chapter Eight, Security Is Where You Find It," and sent it off to several publishers, hinting that other chapters, all as amazing, would be available shortly. Seven form letters, no bites.

With so many rejections, I did what many writers must do. I lowered my sights and used my connections. I sent the story to Mike Rivers who edited a slick local magazine. Mike, an old schoolmate, liked it and sent me fifty dollars. I called him to see if he'd like a story for each issue. He wasn't so sure that I could uncover such stories on a regular basis in the four high rises but said I should try. I was already arranging a collection of these stories for publication as a can't-miss book with sections which had "previously appeared in serial form in Orlando: City of the Worlds," when the first issue hit the newsstands along with an explanation of what I was doing.

The phone started to ring. All of a sudden, everyone in the four buildings was a character with a story that I needed to hear. A lawyer called to tell me about his triplets and the time he spent with them. I should call my story on him "Brian, Byron, Bianca and Dad," he offered. He wouldn't charge for the first interview. A commercial loan officer told me, anonymously of course, that someone in his department had run seven Chicago marathons and I could probably find out who by just asking around. I might even find that runner was available for interviews during his annual leave which started a week from Monday. He knew I'd be interested.

Two government employees, both in "tedious permit-issuing jobs," drove to the bookstore to let me see their paintings. No one knew about their talents yet, you see, because the world wasn't ready for two-sided paintings. They showed me a photograph of the two of them painting at the same time on opposite sides of the canvas. They used themes like "Black and White," "The Child and the Man," and "Two Views of the Same Road." Maybe my article would catapult them to fame. Could I come by their garage next Saturday to see these two sensitivities working in one medium at two sympathetic, yet competing, purposes?

There was more. Four people had apparently saved total strangers from various burning vehicles or residences but had not come forward until now. One woman talked each week with another woman in Nepal using telepathy. A paralegal collected miniature dressers (she knew I'd be fascinated) and had several with working drawers and miniature clothing inside. She also collected samples of elementary-school report cards and felt she had the most complete such collection in the area. I was certain she was right.

When I started receiving résumés with photographs and even story outlines from the hitherto nameless and fameless citizens laboring in my test buildings, I decided my project had been compromised and dropped it. I told myself that my thesis had been proven, my talent was probably modest, and my idea would probably be too easily stolen by other writers. Orlando could just bubble away with its thousands of stories; I was going to be a bookseller.

Besides, the last book publisher to read my proposal, this time fortified with the magazine article, had suggested that if she received "just one more piece on people leading everyday lives who did incredible things after work," she would quit her job, seek out the offending author, and see to it that the FBI set up a dossier on him. The dossier would begin with her anonymous report about the author's secret dealings with an unnamed Central American defense minister. I took her response to be a rejection.

E was gone. It happened on a Thursday and it wasn't supposed to be a surprise. She had told everyone that her last day at Chapters and Verse would be sometime during the week, and we had all assumed it would be Friday. A farewell party was beginning to jell, with staff, some customers, and a few publishers' representatives all invited.

When I opened the store on Thursday, I found E's keys on her desk—my desk—and a note: "I placed one final order last night. It was for some short-story anthologies and some things on the Far East. I thought we were too thin there. I'll write. Keep the doors open and the lights on." That was good-bye from E.

The store seemed very quiet during the day. All the usual things went on: customers came and went, the staff discussed its activities, we talked on the phone. No one would mention E. We talked instead of the unusual quiet. When Evan came in for the evening, he noticed at once that the store radio was not on. He, too, settled into the silence that had descended on Chapters and Verse.

The half-hour before Therese goes home is the only time when all of our full-time staff are in the store together. On that Thursday we found ourselves together at the front counter during that time. Like people who had arranged to meet at a certain place at a certain time, we began discussing the business at hand. I had a list of E's order schedule and other duties which we quickly divided among us. We handed about her responsibilities as carefully as we would handle someone else's prized china. Still we didn't mention E's departure. She was still with us, after all, on the shelves.

That impromptu staff meeting was unusually productive. As a rule, they are disasters. Most end up with someone's feelings hurt, someone totally confused about what has been said, or everyone wondering why such an absurd assembly was arranged in the first place.

The worst of these meetings occurred not long after I took over. I had decided to reorganize our buying by assigning each staff member a section or two to order. Harmon, a part-timer who left us shortly thereafter to become a commercial loan officer, was assigned science fiction and biography because he was the only sci-fi reader on staff, and because he claimed to be writing a biography of ex-governor Claude Kirk. When I noticed that no biographies had arrived in a month's time, I questioned Harmon, who informed me that there just wasn't much in print on the lives of Frank Herbert, Ursula LeGuin, or Isaac Asimov. I nodded and added biography to my own list.

The only decent suggestion to arise from a staff meeting came from Therese. We were struggling with two customers who were, we

54

were positive, purchasing remainders at their reduced price and returning them, under our no-questions-asked policy, for credit at their full price. My solution was to stamp a small symbol, perhaps an "R," on the end papers to prove the book was a remainder at purchase. We'd politely point out the "R" on return and any debate would cease. Therese suggested that we stamp each book discreetly with the word "Liar." Not bad.

We've generally been blessed with excellent staff. Fortunately we rarely have to recruit. Evan and Therese have both been here longer than I have and Christmas helpers usually find us. Somebody always knows somebody for our part-time position.

Last year, though, when we lost Sherry as our full-time receiver, all our somebodies fell through. One woman we hired insisted on leaving her collie outside, tethered to the One Hour Parking signpost. While she worked, she seemed to pine for the poor beast, and I had to ask her to leave since she couldn't manage to extricate herself from her Lassie fog. A young man we tried decided that, no, he really couldn't put up with customers who wouldn't accept his suggestions. "Why do they ask if they don't listen to what I tell them?" he moaned as he left us after two hours. Our third attempt was Susan and she was perfect. She learned quickly, was well read, and would have been ordering our history books for us in no time, if she hadn't left in two weeks. It seems she had accepted two jobs at once and was giving us a test. We must have flunked.

Having struck out on word-of-mouthers, I decided to advertise and interview. Because it is awkward to face customers who "have always wanted to work here" and who are not ever going to be on a list of likely prospects, I cleverly concocted a classified ad omitting our store name: "BOOKSTORE needs retail help. Book knowledge preferred. Send résumé to 4886 Suwannee Road." This was a poor ad and a poor concept. There is only one bookstore in Tangelo at our address, and I had at least four uncomfortable interviews with customers who wanted to work where they shopped. I could tell that each one felt she or he had an inside track, and I could see an enemy list in the making.

My other mistake was that I didn't understand what a code word "résumé" is to the serious job-market player. Résumés are serious, serious business. They came in so polished, professional, and calculating that I understood immediately why we sell so many copies of What Color Is Your Parachute? *Reading them made me realize that packaging now applies not only to cheeseburgers, senators, and* hosiery, but to people who want to work in a place that sells books on packaging.

What's more, there's a new generation of job hunters out there. Many have left their husbands, left their wives, chucked it all to look for a career. The résumés (Did they know we pay seventy-five cents above minimum wage?) were all business. Many started smartly with "OBJECTIVES: growth potential, management, utilize my background and talents in a dynamic industry, etc." To sell science fiction?

They all interviewed well. Not one failed to assure me with a bright smile that "I am a people person."

Checking references on some applicants created surprises. Some had lied and many had stretched dates of employment and responsibilities. Some didn't know they would be undercut by old bosses. For the most part, however, references weren't at the old jobs, having left husband or wives looking for a career.

Then came the sunshine—Lawrence.

Q: What kind of job, if you could pick any, appeals most to you?

A: I want to wake up in the morning and look forward to going to work. I want to go home feeling better yet. That means thinking, reading, and laughing.

Little discussion of salary, some concern over benefits for dependents, a brief conversation about modern poetry, and a discussion of satisfaction. Hiring was immediate.

On the Friday after E left, I was struggling with a phone call. Mr. Tremont was certain that I couldn't understand what book he wanted. "I can't describe it on the phone," he said, "but I know you have it." Having checked the shelves three times already for his volume on France in the 1700s, I knew we did not.

"No, Mr. Tremont. We don't have the book, but we can order it for you. What? No, we really don't have it in stock but we can get it in about a week and then we'll call you. Yes. Yes. I know you'd like to have it today. No. We can order it for you. Mr. Tremont, we can order it for you. No, sir. That is English, English as we speak it here in Tangelo. No, it is not some foreign language translated to mean 'We have your book in the back room.' Good. We'll call you when it gets in. Sounds like an interesting book. Thank you."

I took another call. "Sure, we have some books not on real people. Yes, people but not real people. No, people, not cats or dinosaurs. Right, lots of them are children. I'm sure we have some that won't scare you but a little. Okay, I'll show them to you when you come in. Ask for me. My name is Matt."

Therese was listening in to my end of the conversation. When I hung up, she was laughing. "You sound like E already," she said. For her benefit, I checked my head to see if perhaps I were wearing a hat.

It was nice to hear that—very nice. At that moment I wondered how E could have left this store behind.

You can't look at a stack of books or note cards on a desk in the back room without trying to figure out whose personal clutter it is.

Did Therese put that stack of sailing books near the cooler when she was cleaning out her globe-shaped mug?

Mrs. Hansen's Milton finally came in. I hope whoever received it called her.

Lawrence is the one who keeps ordering Steaming to Bamboola. *Who buys it?*

Evan says, "If we sell a hundred books a day, that means we must order, receive, and put on the front shelves a hundred books a day. This is literature as inventory. If we order only novels by self-conscious writers, this is inventory as literature."

Up front may have books on office arrangements, computerized bookkeeping, Japanese management systems, and small-business record keeping. Back here, a special theory of random order works at every desk.

CHAPTER

9

August 1

Dear Matt,

In Ybor City they used to have readers who shouted their way through various books for workers in the cigar factories. The readers sat on a platform above the work area and called out the literature. That's the kind of fact that is common knowledge for people who know it. For me it is a wonder. Send my first "royalty" check to the Tampa address above and don't forget to order dictionaries for back-to-school.

Most sincerely,

E

Gregory just came in. Gregory. He's always been more or less an object of pity in the area because he's generally perceived to be retarded. Gregory smiles most of the time, talks to no one in particular, and is reputed to have stayed in high school until they graduated him to get rid of him at age twenty-one.

Most of our customers don't notice him anymore. Sometimes the crueler teenagers will giggle or point when he's in, but most people ignore Gregory. Like today, he usually goes to the biography section, takes out a couple of books, and leafs through, page by page. Almost no one thinks he can read, let alone remember what he sees on each page. His eyes move but he goes so fast that he looks like a child overacting the reading of a long assignment.

Nobody cares enough to talk to Gregory, even to call his bluff. Once I asked him if he had enjoyed the Russell Baker autobiography he'd just "read." When he said that he had enjoyed the anecdotes about Baker's various uncles but thought he had detected a certain uneasy smugness later in the book, I knew that Gregory had let me in on some secrets.

Gregory never buys anything. I don't believe he works and don't have any idea how he supports himself. Still I wouldn't trade him for any other customer. He's the only customer we have that, by himself, makes me feel that the store has an important role in the town.

Since he never buys, Gregory usually walks straight out, past the counter, smiling and mumbling. His exiting mumble is really a chant of sorts. He points to the books as he passes, like a priest blessing his flock or a basketball player acknowledging a good pass from a teammate.

"Voices, voices, voices . . ." he chants as he points. It took me several months to understand what the voices are, which is somewhat surprising since I've always heard them myself.

September 3

Dear Matt,

The Gulf Coast is like the small-town festival that too many people hear about. So much has gone wrong here. Sarasota is hard with asphalt and money. Strictly hardbacks and big on the investment books. Send check to me at the rented condominium address above.

Being pursued by the American Dream,

E

Chapters and Verse stopped carrying newspapers a long time before I came because they made little profit and lots of enemies: "Where's my Times? You know I always come in for it!" Since then a small stationary parade of vending machines has grown along the front sidewalk squawking silently about their respective contents—three local papers, the New York Times, two "singles" newspapers, and erratically, something called Power Lights and Vahishi Words.

All but the last seem to sell out each day and at least one woman buys the three locals at once. She's not a book reader so I can't question her about her multiple buys. Though I can't be certain, I think she's looking for errors in recipes so she can claim that she spent several thousand dollars on ingredients and all were wasted since the corn syrup was supposed to be cornstarch, or the t. was supposed to be a T. By now she's probably threatened lawsuits against each paper and only needs to find a sympathetic lawyer to get rolling. Fortunately, in my fantasy, no member of the bar has been hungry enough to take her on as a client. I did see a fellow on TV (three-piece suit with pocket watch in front of a wall full of fake books) claiming "No case too small at Carson's Legal Corporation," so she may have an advocate at anytime.

When the store stopped selling newspapers, Willie Taragon stopped his morning visits. Willie is our town's transient problem. He winters with us, as do several hundred other folks from his end of the economic spectrum. Unlike most big-city transients, though, Willie doesn't return north in summer. In fact he splits the summer months between us and Bryson Beach. He likes Bryson Beach because they have a small Salvation Army shelter and it's rarely crowded that time of year. He also swears the sea breezes are quite cool and help him reflect on our times.

Willie used to come in and read the front pages of several papers each morning. He'd leave his panhandled coffee on our window ledge outside in deference to our policy of NO SOLICITING. NO FOOD, DRINKS, OR SMOKING. NO CHECK CASHING AND VERY LITTLE IN THE WAY OF GOTHIC ROMANCE IN STORE. He would carefully read the top and bottom half of each front page. Periodically he would interrupt his reading to go outside for a sip of coffee. Willie has panache.

The vending machines certainly limit what Willie can know about the world. Now he gets only headlines and half stories. I see him crouching and craning his neck to read another half-inch or so under the fold to see how many died in the fire, or whether the deficit is growing at a faster rate. He seems to care about such things, or at least about getting the full story.

Therese told me that in 1979, Willie was here all year— reading the papers through the machines, holding his morning coffee, and learning half of what had made the world spin the day before. One rainy summer day, she found him sitting in front of a local, bawling. He was cradling an empty coffee cup and staring at the headline: "THE DUKE IS DEAD." You didn't know the half of it, Willie.

61

September 30

Dear Matt,

I'm writing from outside an empty ballpark in St. Petersburg. Ring Lardner probably wrote from the same spot. He probably wrote better, too, but he wasn't as comfortable with the empty park as I am. I like it for what it will allow to happen later.

Haslam's is still here, still outstanding. Maybe you should try to start a used-book section also. Next year. For now get your calendars in and get primed for Christmas so you can keep sending monthly checks to me. Next month, use my St. Petersburg address.

From the quietest spot in Florida,

E

A group of husky young men of various heights came in together this morning. They were all wearing shiny red jackets with white letters proclaiming WISU WRESTLING. I figured they were a traveling wrestling team or, perhaps, a cohesive group of urban guerrillas who had ambushed a traveling wrestling team for their jackets.

Whichever group we were hosting, it was a wonder. Where you might expect a loud, swaggering bunch of immortal braggarts, they were interested in browsing, anxious to share their finds with their compatriots, and quite varied in their reading habits. They were all of an age which is captured only in high-school yearbook pictures. Their faces were unblemished, their souls looking innocently and confidently toward a future which lay somewhere on the high side between heaven and earth. Too old to be dependents and too young to have them, they carried all of our possibilities in their eyes.

Each of the young men made a purchase and each paid with a ten-dollar bill. It seemed that they had taken a per diem which was earmarked for hamburgers, souvenirs, or the movies, and spent a good portion on books. Was it chance that every one of these young fellows felt comfortable buying books while on the road? Did their rooms have no television? Did the coach inspire them to develop mind with body? Whatever combination of teaching, caring, accident, biology, or curiosity makes such events take place, I hope it is widely available.

November 2

Dear Matt,

    Enclosed is a contact print of one of my Jacksonville series. I found these children in front of an old aviation school. The DEMY you see on the picture belongs to Hograd's Air Academy. It now houses the overstock of sweatshirts and plastic alligators for the airport's gift shop. I was surprised when I realized that these are the first children I've photographed since I started. I've been surprised until now by so many adults trying to learn. I can't decide if that phenomenon is a sign of cultural desperation or hope. As booksellers, we must select hope.

    The price of silver must have risen, since film prices are up. Send money, as the college kid is supposed to say. I'm in a cottage in Green Cove Springs, quiet as a TB asylum in the mountains. Christmas will be here soon, O Retailer!

Most sincerely,

E

> *Corporations which order large quantities of single titles are to be commended; they are also required to have written purchase orders, signed by a human being.*
>
> E BAKER

CHAPTER

10

The Terrace Club is our town's version of the type of exclusive organization which judges and other public figures occasionally get blasted for joining. Its membership is strictly limited to men of a particular sex, whites of a particular race, and Americans of a particular Christianity. The club has its own building—a downtown two-story with Spanish architecture, a heavy, hand-worked front door, a brass nameplate outside, no doorbell, and private parking in the rear. No noises from the club can be heard on the outside, ever. If there is, as rumored, a handball court on the roof, it isn't visible from the street, and top-quality black rubber balls have never been known to whistle off the roof onto the street people below.

Happenings inside the club are revealed to outsiders only through gossip, guess, and analysis of decisions presumably made by club members while inside. Power oozes through the stucco to the outside. My own knowledge about the secret inner workings is limited, like most people's, but I have been inside and have even been to a section of the second floor. Last December, perhaps for a party or seminar club members have around Christmastime, the club's full-time manager, Taylor O'Keefe, called me to order some books. Apparently club members and their female support systems were going to treat themselves to culture and self-improvement through reading because he ordered ten copies each of *In Search of Excellence* and *Taking Tea*. I loved it. I arranged with Taylor to call at the club at two o'clock on a Tuesday to deliver the books.

Since the store is only a block from the club, I figured I could bring the books over with a hand truck. When I arrived at the front entrance at two, I was met by Taylor, who swung open the door and invited me in before I could knock.

I have to confess that I was excited by my entrance into an inner sanctum which had been a mystery to me since my childhood. I was also a little put off when I realized that I was out of breath from the walk and therefore a bit on the defensive. I remembered lawyers' offices, professors' studies, and personnel departments, all on second or third floors, all walk-ups. The stair climbing always made my heart race a bit and put me at a disadvantage when I took a seat opposite a well-rested professional.

Since the club's "public" entrance was right on the sidewalk, and since virtually no public parking existed, most visitors had to walk a bit to get to the club and therefore were reminded of their pedestrian qualities. My hand truck further branded me and, for the first and only time I can remember, made me wonder why I had been cast into a class of have-nots. I wasn't happy with this thought and was surprised at myself for thinking it. I haven't since, but I developed instant hostility toward the Terrace Club and Taylor O'Keefe as I tugged my hand truck inside the front door.

Inside, I was all senses. I didn't expect many chances like this one, and I fashioned myself into a combination scout and pool reporter. I was on a foray into secret territory, and I felt a strong obligation to be able to report back my findings to my colleagues on the outside. I sniffed for leather and cigars. I glanced in four directions at once. I remained silent so I could overhear boardroomish chuckles, and strategical discussions about the long-term bond market, or the blackball of some bank vice-president.

Several feet inside the front door, a dark wooden breakfront extended to the left and right about fifteen feet in each direction. The breakfront prohibited anyone in the entrance foyer, or anyone passing by on the sidewalk and glancing through an open front door, from seeing anything but oak paneling. The Terrace Club was, in this respect, in a league with most adult nightclubs and any restaurant bathroom built to code. You might look in the door, but you wouldn't see anything. I looked for sign-in books, two-way mirrors, antique hat hooks, gaudy ashtrays, pictures of old members, or anything else of interest in the entranceway. I found nothing. Taylor led me to the left.

I was prepared to enter a sitting room full of red leather chairs worthy of Alistair Cooke, or at least a room full of Nigels and Reginalds, but found only a staircase. The stairs were carpeted in Spanish-style hotel red and black and I knew that my hand truck would mar the carpet. I left it behind and hefted the box of books to my hip. Taylor didn't offer to help. Since the staircase was narrow and the books too heavy to carry in front of me, I climbed sideways to the second floor.

I was a curious and angry servant by the time I found myself in a kitchen area much like most church kitchens I'd seen—white and aluminum, clean and organized. I assumed it would soon be abuzz with preparations for a Christmas feast to be topped off with gifts of my books. Judging by an incredible wall of liquor off to my right, Terrace Club members must toast the holidays after every course and then drink in honor of most everything else.

Taylor asked me to put the books on a counter. I was stacking them up when a phone rang and Taylor disappeared downstairs. A detective's delight! I headed through the kitchen door that led to "out there." The dining room was dark, with its maroon rug bordered by a sedate stretch of dark oak floor. There were no pictures on the dark brown paneled walls. How could these people enjoy parties surrounded by unbroken brown?

In the center of the room were four long dining tables, again heavy wood. They were arranged in a box pattern so there could be no head or foot. The arrangement also dictated that dinner conversation be limited to those sitting side by side, since no one was sitting just across from anyone else. Everyone ate while staring into the vacuum created at the center of the box. Maybe someone danced in the middle, maybe some well-dressed and well-soused couple hurdled a table to take a seat inside on the floor, or maybe the dirty dishes were tossed into a heap in the center. I was reminded of the game of Clue. It was done in the Dining Room, by Colonel Mustard, using a copy of *In Search of Excellence*. What was done?

I noticed a pair of french doors at the opposite end of the room. Since no one had said "Don't wander," I wandered through them. The room I entered, the last new one I was to see in the club, was glassed in on two sides and paneled in the familiar oak on the other two. I'd never noticed any windows in the club before and resolved to look for them once outside to pinpoint my location. I've never seen them from the outside, although I don't search all that hard since I like a little mystery now and again.

Except for six padded chairs, three facing out along each glassed wall, the room was empty. The chairs were high backed and were anchored to the floor on posts so they could swivel. Like the dining-room chairs, they weren't arranged for easy conversation.

When I took a seat in one, I learned their purpose. In front of each was a telescope. The telescopes weren't the skinny, carefully calibrated, serious types used by scientists. Instead they were the heavily encased type made available to tourists at SCENIC VIEW—ONE MILE. States with mountains have lots of them, but the only ones I'd seen in Florida were on top of the old Citrus Tower, where you used to be able to pay a quarter and spend a minute or two looking at thousands of rows of orange trees.

The six telescopes didn't have quarter slots and I didn't hesitate to look through the one in front of me. It was focused out beyond the bypass on an old building which had been a foundry way back when. It had never been occupied during my memory. Investigator that I was, I scooted over to the next seat and squinted to see what its telescope had captured. The foundry building appeared again. A third telescope also peered at the foundry, and I could see the vines strangling its walls and reaching for its rotted roof. The roof itself had several holes, welcoming rain and birds or whatever else wished to enter the building.

The find was so intriguing that theories competed for attention in my mind: The foundry held gold. The foundry would be razed for a truck terminal. A new university was planned for the foundry site. Laundered money was exchanged there. Terrace Club members met there at midnight for their fun. Then Taylor appeared at the door and, stealing words from countless poorly written movies, grunted, "Hey! What are you doing in there?"

There are lines drawn in life. Some things are forbidden to some people, and something is forbidden to each of us. Clearly, entrance into this observatory had been forbidden to Taylor. He was astounded by my audacity but, for himself, refused to set foot in the room. I had gained a psychological advantage over him, not to mention some knowledge he probably didn't have.

As I joined him in the dining room and then the kitchen, I became the businessman. I presented the invoice, thanked him for the order, and left. Payment was not offered me in the club, which served to corroborate the generally held belief that common currency and even checks were not to change hands in the building. A check was mailed that day.

Following my hand truck back to Chapters and Verse, I knew some things.

Our business is short on the perquisites of executive life. In a high-powered corporate world full of club memberships, management meetings in idyllic mountain retreats, and diesel luxury sedans, independent bookselling is surely looked on as a disgrace. We seem to have only one advantage that comes with the territory—readers' copies.

These paper martinis come in a variety of finishes from signed first editions to poorly bound, uncorrected galley proofs. The best ones show up at home. They're always unexpected, though many of them have been sent at the request of the publisher's representative who has asked me which books I want to review. Somehow, as I rip the staples out of the padded mailing envelope, I always feel I've been singled out by the publisher to read this particular book. I must admit that I do promote books I get as readers' copies since I read most of them out of interest or gratitude.

Many publishers historically have sent readers' copies to buyers' homes to emphasize, I suppose, that these books are to be read by the buyer and not to be placed in the store for sale. I don't face a moral dilemma over whether to bring them to the store to sell for a clean $19.95 profit. I don't even consider that act of heresy. No, my only decision is choosing which relative will get the books when I am finished.

There are only two choices, Aunt Lucille and DeWitt. My only other living relative is my mother. She, however, reads mostly books by authors whose last name starts with an "A," since a palm reader in Cassadaga told her that someone with a name starting with that letter had secretly written her life. She's been on a search since then to find the right book to learn about her future.

She was terrified after rereading Little Women *and spent $2,500 on lab tests for Beth's disease. She stopped only when she received a personal letter from the president of her health-insurance company begging her to read the results of any of the tests she had undergone so she could pronounce herself well enough to sign on with another insurer. When she finished* Clan of the Cave Bear, *she carried herself with a new sense of dignity. She almost went off the deep end, though, when she finished an Italian novel about a woman who drowned all her cats in the Adriatic because they wouldn't fetch things for her. She denies all of this but does admit to taking her reading more seriously than most. Clearly, giving her a book, even a readers' copy, would be too much of a responsibility, so I restrict myself to Aunt Lucille and DeWitt.*

Lucille will read anything, anything free. She used to read, cover to cover, handouts from the Scientologists, encyclopedias from grocery stores, those neon-covered hardbacks given out by various robed and zombied airport cultists, countless Bibles, and even old textbooks given away each year by the school board.

When I started getting readers' copies, everything changed for her. Her standards rose at once when she learned that I would receive, gratis, books of all types. She began to read fiction, biography, cookbooks and business books. She read the Encyclopedia of Golf *and became conversant with real estate when I received five books from a publisher specializing in those get-rich-quick-from-land-,-I-did books.*

She reads everything and that's the problem with Aunt Lucille. She cannot be satisfied. She visits me at home now that she knows that literature appears in my mailbox. She's often around when I get home to help me go through my mail. She wants first crack at everything, but so do I. I've decided that she can't be insulted, however, so I usually tell her that I want to read the book first so I'll know whether to order it. "I am the intended reader," I like to tell Aunt Lucille.

She's patient, though. When she loses out on the first shot, she reminds me of the books that came last time she visited. She figures that I must have finished with them since I'm demanding to read the newest arrivals, so she opens her bottomless purse for me to insert the "old stuff." To her credit Aunt Lucille returns every book. Timely returning of borrowed books is an indication of excellent character.

DeWitt, on the other hand, isn't an eclectic reader. He only likes fiction, only sagas, and only sagas which are over four hundred pages long. As a book grabber, therefore, he's not any competition for Aunt Lucille or for me, since I stay away from any book that spans generations in its cover blurb. Give DeWitt a novel set in seven cities and covering the trials of a family from its humble origins in the tin mines of Cornwall through development of an internationally successful cosmetics firm, and he's ready to disappear for a week or so while he lives with the family. No one could appreciate the opportunity to escape with such company more than DeWitt, a bachelor at seventy-three who is Aunt Lucille's neighbor and cousin. Though DeWitt isn't interested in most of my readers' copies, he does come running when I call him with titles like Leah's Clan, Brothers and Cousins, *or* The Pride of the Winthrops.

In his way, DeWitt causes more problems for me than does Lucille. He's a talker and the single most frequent visitor to the store. Probably out of some misguided interest in helping the "family business," he finishes a saga and comes into the store to hawk it. He parks himself a section away from the shelf holding his latest conquest and waits until someone wanders near. Then, with the quickness of a good British playwright, he pounces on unsuspecting customers with a five-minute summary of the book he feels they, too, should devour. He has thought through his presentation, usually summarizing the book by generation, weaving major themes, and noting certain characters that the buyer must certainly study. All the while, he waves his readers' copy up and down like a male peacock strutting his stuff before a helpless hen. Most buyers are polite after their initial surprise. Few buy the book, however, and DeWitt ranks somewhere below the authors' collector cards on my list of successful promotion techniques.

Still, circulating readers' copies is like the mysterious sweetness of passing notes in school, or sharing cold water from a metal cup on a scorching Florida summer day.

Where else would you buy a calendar but in a bookstore?

E BAKER

CHAPTER

11

December 1

Dear Matt,

I'm still near Jacksonville. I can't decide if this city is trying to fight off the growth everywhere to the south, or if the developers are just fighting each other so hard that they're all losing. Whatever the reason, the city isn't exploding quite like others we know well, and that's probably for the best. The office buildings here are tall, though. They gawk above the river and the city like gangly deacons watching infighting at committee meetings.

The holiday season should be on you. Don't you feel like a smart merchant? Don't you already wish you had thirty more copies of this or that $29.95 hardback? Has the lady from Wisconsin sent a check for a gift certificate for Clare Morrison? She will, and it will mark the official kickoff of Christmas at Chapters and Verse.

I may go further south soon, but when you can stop running for a minute, send yet another check, yet another time to me at the same address.

Did you know I had a sister? Her name is Margaret Day Baker-Pierce. Maybe you should add her to the store mailing list. Her address is attached with her calling card. She's trying to revive the calling-card tradition. I say leave a dead card lay. Regards to the staff.

Happy holidays,

E

I once read a story about a couple who lived in a tiny apartment, had no friends, and were allowed to work only a few hours a week. Like most people in their society, they kept a lifetime's supply of food in pill form, and virtually never left their home or each other's side. To keep some interest in their lives, they learned to interpret the slightest changes in each other. He noticed when a single hair spoiled her otherwise perfect part, or when she pronounced a word with a different inflection than she had used years before. She could tell when he was upset, or whether he had coughed earlier in the day by noting pauses between his words which were milliseconds longer than usual.

They would probably not be good company for dinner and a movie for anyone the least bit self-conscious, but what else could they do for kicks? The story isn't much except for its lesson about creating a world from detail.

If you want to learn about Therese, Lawrence, and Evan, you have to study carefully what they do. At first glance they may seem similar. They each know most every book that's shelved here, and each harbors a cache of trivia no different in scope than that of anyone on any job: "We got in three copies of that Hawaiian shirt book and sold them all in one morning." "The science encyclopedia is $97.95." "When Richard Brautigan died, we couldn't find a single book of his at the wholesaler." Each of them can gift wrap a book in less than thirty seconds, and they apply the same criterion in deciding whether to grant a shopping bag to people making large purchases.

The important details are more subtle. These are the small motions of each of them as they find a book and present it for sale. If you ask Evan for help finding a book, you may notice a second or two in which he looks at you, and then beyond you, before leading the way to the appropriate section. I'm sure he's asking why you requested what you did, who you are, and whether you are choosing wisely. He silently asks and answers all these questions about as fast as those postal workers who have to recognize zip codes and dispatch letters at some incredible rate.

These human zip-code scanners, however, don't get involved with the thousands of envelopes parading in front of them. If you study Evan's face as he heads toward your book, you may see a slight pursing of the lips, the beginnings of a smile, or the raised eyebrows of resignation. He's concerned about anyone who cares enough to ask him for help. Busy times seem to make him a bit cross, possibly because his normal analysis time is short-circuited.

When Evan sells a book, he drops it to the bag's bottom as if to test the strength of the paper. For him the transaction was over when he finished matching book, customer, and motive.

Lawrence, on the other hand, places his emphasis on the book itself. Ask for help finding a biography, for instance, and he'll lead you to the book you need like a tour guide building you up for a sudden view of the Parthenon. He'll probably pull the book from the shelf for you and present it to you like a ring bearer offering up the ring on a pillow. He'll watch your hands grasp the book before he lets go. As he heads back to the counter, he'll look back to see that the book and you are getting along all right. Somehow he carries off this apparent overkill so pleasantly that he annoys no one and, indeed, no one seems to notice his protective feelings toward the books themselves.

At checkout time, Lawrence is one of those who chooses carefully the appropriate bag size and lays his selection on the counter next to the purchase. Then he lifts up the top edge of the bag, stoops down a bit, and squints as he slides the book in. No matter what the book, he treats each one as a jeweler does an expensive necklace.

Therese dons a special business look when she's working with a customer. It's quite unlike her expression when doing a window or shelving new arrivals. In those two situations, she's likely to be smiling at herself as if telling herself some secret. With customers, she has a shallower smile, a business smile.

Therese's always aware of the store, the merchandise, the customer, and the transaction. She has established a cycle for ringing up a sale, making change, tearing off the receipt from the register tape, checking it, placing it on top of the books, placing books and receipt in the bag, and handing the works to the customer with the bag top folded down. I've never known her procedure to change, except around Christmas when someone is helping her during the busiest times. She doesn't like such help and seems a little less sure of herself when she can't control the complete cycle.

Chapters and Verse itself is a mass of changing detail. The books change, the stock levels swell and shrink, customers rotate, and the front windows are continually in flux. From time to time, new small areas appear to me; areas which have been here all along, but which my eye has passed over. I've been surprised by unused spaces on columns, a wasted corner between Best-Sellers and New Fiction, and an empty spot below the fuse box. Customers age, reading habits change, and the view from behind the counter evolves.

December 24

Dear Matt,

Christmas Eve on St. Augustine Beach: not an oxymoron exactly, but not the real thing, either. Don't I remember something about snow and home and hearth?

I just returned from a walk on the beach. There were no stars, but the moon did a magical job, frosting the waves. No one walks on the beach on Christmas Eve, but I didn't mind being alone. I could imagine William humming and Chapters and Verse buzzing and even a happy chorus of Corb Sams, Therese, Gregory, Stephen, and the rest. You sang bass rather sheepishly at first and then got interested and more bold.

Your present is on the table here. You didn't need to remember me this way, but of course that's why you did. I had a good eye back then when you were at that tie place. What did you learn there? Did women buy ties with more color?

Yes, your present is on the table here. I'm touching the bow now. Tied like a knot—a Windsor knot perhaps, since I don't know one tie knot from another and have such good thoughts about the Windsor.

Matthew Mason! Your present just made its way into my hands. Hold on a minute.

I like the box. Hold on a minute.

Too much tissue, too much anticipation.

Where, oh where, did you find this exquisite box? It's a small bookcase! Best of all, it's already filled. A pocket atlas, a guide to the Keys, Cézanne, I. M. Pei, Cajun cooking . . . What's the pattern? Hold on a minute.

Still thinking.

Aha! Something from every section, right? It has to be. Wait. You forgot sports. No, here's *The Boys of Summer*.

I have a traveling bookstore now. Sort of a literary shrine I can set up on the dressers and nightstands of the motels I'm staying in.

Never have I had such a perfect Christmas present and it comes on just the right evening. Thank you, thank you.

And thanks again, dear Matthew,

E

If you spend your days thinking life is all cool winds and bookstores, you're either callous or incredibly inattentive. That's not to say that you can't be an optimist, but there are even now, realtors out on the bypass and thunderstorms brewing in the Gulf.

MATTHEW MASON

CHAPTER

12

Stand on one end of Suwannee Road and look down the sidewalk at about eleven o'clock on any morning in the week after New Year's Day. One by one, you'll see us shopkeepers come out of our front doors, pretending to seek only a breath of fresh winter air. We'll stretch, we'll look left and right, and then we'll sneak a look over to the public parking lot across the street. Finally we'll look at each other without talking and go back inside.

That's what merchants' fear looks like to the civilian. If you could hear what is singing in our minds, it would probably sound like some familiar and plaintive lyrics: ☺"Who will buy my cable-knit sweaters? Who will buy my new hardbound books? Someone must need a new reflex camera. Someone needs paint . . ." The year's curtain always goes up with the same opening number.

One by one, we review the slow morning, the quiet we told our families we would see this day and week. There is nothing wrong with the quiet; we're doing nothing wrong, and no one is doing any better. Last week was good, but last week was last year. Who cares about last year? Why must every new year start so evilly slow? The questions and doubts stampede the block. We will take them home to our neat rooms where everything is shelved and everything is cleaned on a schedule. The fear will rumble home with us, and the children will know these are days when they can't ask who came in that they know. The children will go outside and wonder: Who will watch me ride my new scooter? Who will read my dinosaur books? Someone must be back from vacation. Someone must want to play.

That's the way this week should be. Without it there would be no better weeks.

I was supposed to be in the back room, welcoming three boxes of Penguin Classics to Tangelo. I'd already placed Hawthorne, Flaubert, and Machiavelli on the receiving counter when I decided it was time to sample that fresh air out on the sidewalk.

While I was in front of the store, pacing like my neighboring retailers in harness and worrying about most everything, Irv Tyson came by. He was usually with Corb Sams and the woman I don't know, but this time he was alone.

Irv and I had spoken in the store, but never for more than a few minutes. Though he is younger than I am, he has always seemed older because he is so comfortable with himself. It is not that he isn't curious about things the way others his age are; it is more that he isn't in a hurry. He could be smug, given his position as a very young, wealthy retiree, but he is not. On this particular day, he immediately noticed my own uneasiness.

"Things get slow after the holidays, don't they?" he asked me. "This is your first since E went on her merry way to wherever she went on her way. I bet that's a strange feeling."

I mumbled something which probably confirmed his suspicions about my condition on that morning, because he suggested that I should get away from the store for a while. "I'm going to look at an old building south of town. Why don't you come along, walk through it with me, and then we'll catch some lunch at Anson's. I like company and you look like you need some."

When I asked which building had his interest, Irv said it was the foundry. Since there was this matter of the telescopes at the Terrace Club to decipher, I had to go. It crossed my mind that Irv might have some connection to the club and might have talked to Taylor O'Keefe, its gatekeeper. Perhaps they thought I might be in the way of someone's plans for the old structure. No matter, I was still intrigued and was also happy to get away for a few hours. Lawrence said, "Go, please."

We were at the foundry in about ten minutes. What we saw was a building which had stood about as long as it possibly could without some help. The walls seemed ready to fall into the interior, and I feared just touching one of them would bring down the works. Whitened bricks over the door indicated that the foundry had once been called Florida Forge.

78

Irv had told me that the building was originally a wooden structure. "It was probably built as a foundry in the late 1800s and maybe remodeled to do something else after that. I don't remember anything ever going on in here in my lifetime, and I don't think my parents ever mentioned any action in the place, either." Irv's family had been in Tangelo long enough that they would know about every building with any years on it.

The front door was open slightly. Irv and I squeezed through without opening it further. We entered a large room. It was lit by clouded sunlight sifted through two small windows and several openings in the roof. The room was empty except for a stack of lumber against the back wall.

"There are only three rooms," he said before we'd proven that by a short tour. "This big one was the foundry itself. The molds were kept in here and all the heating and pouring were done over by this vented area."

Irv showed me around as if he'd been there hundreds of times, although he swore he'd never been inside.

We made our way around the big room. The floor had apparently once been made of fitted red bricks. Many of the bricks had been removed years ago for new work in other buildings so that the floor was mostly dirt with a few remaining patches of brick.

"Look over here," Irv said. "This raised area was probably the supervisor's station, and that double-brick area may have held the heaviest equipment or vats." Irv found two pieces of lumpy silver metal and showed them to me.

"What was this place producing anyway?" I wanted to know more since I liked the idea of being in a relatively undisturbed part of Tangelo's history. We were urban archaeologists. I convinced myself that I could see heat marks on some bricks, and that I had found some sort of drain in a side wall.

"Probably it had something to do with citrus," Irv said. "Everything did back then. Maybe it made nails for the fruit crates or metal bands to go around them."

"Everything was citrus related?"

"Just about, except the things which served the people who came here for reasons related to the groves, like the railroad. This place is on an old spur. You can see where a car actually came to the middle of this room, probably after being removed from a train behind the building. I suppose it brought raw metal in and the nails or another product back out. Maybe the foundry got work from the larger factories that built the trains themselves. There were a bunch of car shops around here, you know."

I didn't know that. Why would Irv know? I had grown up here but knew very little about the beginnings of Tangelo. Irv, who had spent his youth up north in boarding schools, seemed to know every detail, every most likely possibility. "What were the other two rooms?" I wanted to know.

"I have no idea," Irv said.

We headed for the closest room which was at the front of the foundry. It, too, was empty. Its window, now devoid of glass, faced a small Florida house across the street. "That was E Baker's house until she left," Irv said. I had forgotten that she had lived out this way. Now I wondered if he had brought me here because he was curious about E and wanted to use the house as an excuse to ask me about her.

When I told him I'd never seen her house, he suggested we go over and look at it. "It's been vacant since she left," he said. "No one is trying to rent it, and I haven't checked to see who has title to it. Maybe E has kept it."

"I don't think so. She told me she had always been a renter and that the business was the only thing she'd ever owned besides a string of Chryslers. Let's look at the last room here before we go over to the house," I suggested. I hadn't learned enough about the foundry yet.

A door in the small room in which we stood was the only entrance into the third room. That door, a metal one, was locked. The handle on our side wobbled when I pulled it and would have fallen off had I pulled harder. We had no key and no way to pry open the door, so we left an investigation of that room for another day. I noticed when we were once again outside that there were no windows in that third room. So many children's books, mysteries, and horror stories depend on mysterious rooms like that, I thought.

Walking along the front of the foundry, I saw a surveyor's stake with a strip of red plastic on it. Corresponding stakes were placed at the far end of the building's front and at the rear of the building along the side. Someone had recently surveyed the property.

I wanted to know what Irv knew about the foundry. I was certain he knew more than he'd said. He was, after all, connected to the kind of money that could, as they say, "control" certain pieces of real estate. More important, it had been his idea that we come here. Whether or not he'd tell me what he knew, or whether he'd be insulted by the question, I didn't know.

"Irv. Who owns this place?" I had learned something from E about being direct.

"Corb has an option of sorts to buy it from a guy in South Carolina whose family has owned it since the thirties."

"What's Corb doing with it?"

"You'd have to ask him. I have a theory, though."

"Let me hear it. Only tell me what Corb is doing investing in property. He's always acted like he's not knee-deep in money and not at all interested in changing his situation."

"Well, I don't think it's his money. I think he's helping someone else buy the place, or at least hold off a third party from buying it."

"I don't get it."

"See, there's all kinds of interest in this place right now. I think it's just because someone got interested, surveyed it, and other people are trying to figure out who's up to what."

"And Corb?"

"You know Corb. He just likes to be in the thick of things. I think he senses that there are some competing forces at work, and he just has a taste for the action. Have you ever known him to stay out of an argument?"

"No. He lives for them. But what are the opposing sides here?"

"I don't know all of it, so I'd probably just mislead you if I took a stab at explaining. If I knew who surveyed the place to begin with, I'd know better what was going on. For now all I know for certain is that Corb has to either buy the place in ninety days or lose the money he put up for the option. He won't tell me what he's doing or for whom."

"What does Corb do anyway?"

"He owns two small groves and pretends to fill his time as his own caretaker. The truth is that he's got two hearty groves which even he can't seem to kill off, so he makes his money on them every year—not a lot, just enough to keep him from having to work full-time. He knows his limits, though. He wouldn't stretch too thin for this foundry building. He's using someone else's money."

Irv and I crossed the street to E's house. It was a small home with no features to distinguish it from thousands of other Florida homes built after World War II except for its front yard. Though E had been gone, and the house abandoned for several months, the yard was in perfect shape. That was because it consisted of nothing but cactus and stones. Most people would have said that such a yard was consistent with E's personality, but I remembered her saying that she had never touched her yard in all the years she'd lived in her house and was thankful for that. I doubt she noticed it.

It is impossible to walk past the windows of a vacant home and not look in. Irv and I looked in the front window. We saw only an empty living room and hallways to the other rooms. Irv headed around to the back while I stayed in front trying to imagine E seated in that living room. I doubted she had had a television. There were no built-in bookcases and no furniture had been left behind. For all I could tell, the room had always been empty and E had used it only for pacing.

Irv called to me to come around to the back. "Look through here," he said, pointing through a back window. I could see all the way through the small house, sighting through the front window and across the street to the foundry. This had been E's view from her living room.

Then I noticed what had caught Irv's eye. On the wall of the living room, right next to the window, was a painted duplicate of the window and its view. E had painted exactly what she could see in the daytime, perhaps so she could view it at night.

Apparently, she had painted the foundry view earlier in the year, since her rendering included leaves on the two crape myrtles which now stood bare in front of the foundry. I hadn't known she could paint at all.

While I was thinking about the painting and how strange a view E had fashioned for herself, Irv said he was hungry. We left for Anson's.

We had a bookbinder next door for about ten months. Before that, there was an eight-foot alley between our store building and the beauty parlor. Richard Todds, our landlord, sensed this awful vacuum should be filled, so he wriggled a building permit out of the town council and proceeded to roof over the space and stick a glass front on it. An eight-by-eighty space didn't appeal to many retailers, and Richard "held on" to the space for over a year until Mo Samuels showed up.

Mo came in to see me before he moved into town. "I want to bind books," he said right off and proceeded to tell me that he wanted a place to settle, set up shop, and stay forever. He had a passion for the craft, had studied with a master craftsman in Vienna, and would take on only the jobs he wanted. He had no family, no interest in having one, and wished only for a modest living offering enduring, beautiful books.

"If I can do the few things that I do well, that's more than most people ever do. I don't need to franchise my business, add on a printing branch, or sell time on a copy machine," he said.

We had lunch together and he wanted to know if we had calls for books to be mended or Bibles to be rebound, and if we had any serious book collectors in Tangelo. I told him we did, and he wanted to know about nearby space. I explained that what looked like an architectural mistake next door was really a storefront and sent him to see Richard Todds.

From the day Mo opened Emperor Bookbinders, he proved true to his words. I knew from my regular customers that he turned down certain jobs, like repairing briefcases or preparing bound graduation certificates. The work he took in was done beautifully. He repaired a copy of The Call of the Wild for me that I thought was beyond help. It's a treasure now, rather than a sad treasure. No one ever complained about his binding.

Mo seemed happy. We'd meet for lunch every Thursday, a routine that grew naturally out of our first lunch. He talked mostly of his craft. Though I had handled books by the thousands, I learned how little I knew about the physical construction of these miracles.

Once, after Mo noticed how ignorant I was when the talk turned technical, he pulled out a book and gave me an anatomy lesson. With the aid of the gold burnisher he always carried, he took me on a loving tour through the book from a binder's viewpoint. I discovered a world of front boards, headbands, fore edges, heads, and tails I'd never thought about.

Lunch by lunch, he taught me to appreciate the beautiful results of his essentially primitive art with its handmade papers, special glues and cloth, and demand for patience. I learned to recognize quarter binding and developed an affinity for elegant leather half binding. Mo didn't seem to favor gilding a book's edges, so I didn't learn much about that. I did pick up enough in those lunches that Mo presented me with a bone folder, wrapped in flannel, and the note, "So now you're ready to try your own hand?"

Mo also talked about his ex-wife, or rather his fights with his ex-wife. He recounted phenomenal and insidious attacks that would make Edward Albee jealous. He told me how Francine would goad him to be more ambitious and then would discourage him from taking binding classes. She would set up interviews for him for "real jobs," usually involving accounting of some sort, since she wished to be a CPA's wife. Unbeknownst to Mo, she'd even written letters to accounting firms, offering him for trainee positions and signing his name.

One time her letters were so persuasive that Mo was offered, sight unseen, an assistant auditor's job in a second-level firm. Francine was beside herself when Mo refused to show up for work and proceeded to shut the ingrate out of their kitchen and bathroom for a week. Mo retaliated by eating huge hoagy sandwiches in their bedroom. These were laden with garlic, peppers, and assorted odorous and spicy meats. He developed ready access to their neighbors' bathroom by telling them that Francine had a "certain delicate problem" which required, according to their family physician, that no one else use the same facilities. When the neighbors sent her a get-well card citing a jailed uncle who suffered from the same sad disease, Francine became more angry and the battle escalated. Soon the weapons included various plumbing tools, trick sheets, venomous notes left on pillows, and the kind of cheap gags that no one on earth has ever felt were funny. None of this ugly pettiness seemed to fit the Mo that I had lunch with each week.

Mo never took that job as an auditor's assistant and resisted all of Francine's attempts to wrap his hands about an accountant's pencil. He wanted to bind fine books and pleaded with Francine to understand. He took her to the university library, introduced her to the binder, and even presented her with her own family Bible rebound by his teacher. She wasn't moved and only laughed at him when he headed for his makeshift workshop to practice his beloved art.

The height of Francine's cruelty came when she locked him in his workshop for two days, after removing his tools. On her regular visits to give him food and scold him for being a dreamer with "an unprofitable and dying non-profession," he pleaded for his tools, not for his release. He got both when Francine left, filing for divorce with a lawyer who was studying for his CPA exam at night.

Mo was doing what he wanted at Emperor Bookbinders. Unfortunately he was not earning even a modest living at his trade, so he was forced to close. He accepted a job with the state library.

On the Saturday before Mo was to leave, I walked next door to give him a going-away gift. I'd found a leather-bound blank book with handmade end papers, a leather box, and a finely woven page marker sewn into the binding. Mo greatly admired the work as he walked through it at his front counter. His gold burnisher peeked out from his shirt pocket as he ran his hands along the spine, inspected the stitching, and sniffed the leather on the book. I thought he seemed the slightest bit disappointed when he realized that each page was blank, but I might have been wrong.

When he had finished inspecting the book and thanking me, he asked me into his workroom for a cup of coffee. The workroom was hidden from the front counter area and, in the few seconds it took to walk behind the counter and through the opening to it, I realized that I'd never asked or been invited to see it before. From all the information about bookbinding that Mo had shared with me, I felt I knew what was going to be there. I knew of the stacks of pressed leather, the neatly stored knives and glue brushes, and the wall racks of special rubbing, crimping, and chiseling tools. I could envision a stack of tattered books at one end of a long worktable, and a smaller stack of completed, bound books at the other. These last would probably be individually wrapped in tissue and placed on the green felt that would be inset in the table.

Between the two stacks would be the tools, some strips of brass, stacks of assorted cardboards, papers, and cloth, and the book currently being repaired. In the front of the work area, close to the sales counter so Mo could easily reach his customers, would be an old wooden desk. It would be neat and would feature two or three examples of Mo's best work, work he couldn't bear to sell. It would also have a shelf of a dozen or so classics on bookbinding, all ironically in need of repair. We'd laugh about that.

I was right about the desk. That's all. The rest of the workroom was empty except for a flatbed wooden cart at the rear next to the receiving door. The cart held a half-dozen packages, wrapped and labeled for shipping, each the size of a single book and each addressed to Mo from a different bindery. Mo sent his work out.

I was terrified to contemplate Mo's shame when he saw I had learned his secret, but his expression of calm made it clear that he felt nothing unusual. As we drank our coffee, talked of Mo's impending move, and I heard one last story about Francine putting yeast in his binding glue, I realized that Mo had been doing no more or less than he had said he would. He took in only the jobs he wanted, provided only the best product, and never expanded his business beyond his beloved craft.

Buying a book is like selecting a dinner companion
except that the risks and prospects are far greater.
CORB SAMS

CHAPTER   January 9

13

Dear Matt,

It's the middle of the year, not New Year's. I'm a bit tired of traveling but, since I gave up my house, I'm not able to yearn for home. Home now is an assortment of road habits mixed with things I like to remember. I do miss the bookshelves, my reading chair, the thud of the morning's paper being delivered, and the occasional evening phone call. No complaints, though; I resolved to live without these pleasures when I hit the road with my single-lens reflex.

I just began looking at my work after five months of photography in hopes that some trends or theme would emerge. I suspect that today isn't a good day to start looking, since the only thing I've noticed is that humans, when they are learning anything from how to iron clothing to how to read the clouds, tend to do so with their mouths open. What can that mean?

Just to humor me, send me your December sales total along with my check . . . Ormond Beach address above.

Here's to the New One,

E BAKER

When he first came in this evening, I think I heard Evan singing "Sweeten my coffee with a morning kiss," but it might have been "I've often wished for a girl like this." Either way, he could be in love. Of course it may have been "Try Hormel ham, on bread, with swiss," in

87

which case television advertising has damaged the music cells in his
remaining brain parts so that he can only sing commercial refrains,
with feeling.

For months I have speculated on Evan's out-of-store life, but I
haven't formulated a theory I like. I used to analyze him by the books
he took home under our staff borrowing policy. Once, he borrowed
Moe Berg, an unsatisfying biography about a fascinating and
mysterious man, which we've kept on the shelves much too long at my
insistence while waiting for a buyer. I decided that Evan took it
because he'd never heard of Berg and hated the idea that there were
people important enough to merit biographies whom he'd never heard
about. Next he took Wisconsin Death Trip, so I advanced my
theory to cast Evan as a budding mystic.

I threw out these early ideas when he bundled up these three
titles for reading at home: We All Make Mistakes, 1001 After
Dinner Jokes to Make the Rotarians Guffaw, and Robert's Rules
of Order. These books stressed the obvious, the tested, and the
rational, and didn't fit my earlier ideas about Evan.

I abandoned my analysis by book choice completely when he
began taking home only books dealing with the history and philosophy
of science. Evan remains a mystery, but I do hope he's in love.

I lasted two weeks before I had to see the foundry's third
room. It wasn't my fault; I could have left well enough alone,
but I was working in the evening when this young, rich couple
walked in. Their combined age was fifty-four or fifty-six or
some even number, since even their ages must have matched.
He bought the *Robb Report* with comfort. That is, he didn't look
inside first. She placed *Abitare* on top of his magazine at the
checkout and reached, without fumbling, into a small leather
purse to extract a credit-card folder.

Unlike virtually all the regulars, these two did not discuss
their pending purchases with each other or even glance at the
other's magazine. He was self-confident khaki; she was
tastefully red, black, and white. So young to wear money so
well, they left for an evening.

This mysterious couple left me wanting an evening myself.
The moon was full, my calendar was empty, and the foundry
was still not completely explored. It was closing time.

Before I knew it, I found myself parked in front of E's old
house, looking at the front of the foundry. An old Chevy was

parked just up the street, probably abandoned like the building. The moon lit up the foundry's bricks with their Florida Forge message. The front door stood just open as before.

In I went, explaining to who ever might discover me inside that I'd been here before with Irv and thought maybe I'd left behind my jacket. The moonlight washed the floor and walls of the large room with a yellow gray. I couldn't see much, but this wasn't the room I was interested in anyway.

I headed for the small room I'd been in with Irv. It was even darker than the first with just the single, small window to let in the evening light. I was scolding myself for not bringing along a flashlight when I saw a pencil-thin line of white on the far wall where the metal door was. The light had to be coming from the third room, and that should have been my signal to retreat.

I didn't. As I walked across the room toward the strip of light, I blamed my mother for this temporary irrationality and roguery. She was the one who believed in spirits and fate. If it were up to her, she would be calling out to whoever or whatever was in the light, probably asking for a sign about her future. Not me. I walked as quietly as I could on the dirt floor between me and the light.

The door was barely open, allowing that thin ribbon of light along its edge. My elementary knowledge of optics told me that I could probably look through the door without being detected since there was darkness behind me. That would work as long as I made no noise and whoever was in the room did not wish to leave it. There was no question that I was going to look.

Standing in the dark, squinting to see through the door's opening, I saw a room full of light and color. The walls had been freshly painted in white, a red wooden decking made a new floor, and several yellow-and-blue platforms were placed here and there. The ceiling was black, but it held two rows of track lights which illuminated every part of the room and highlighted each of the platforms.

Stephen, from the Windsor, was seated on one of the platforms. He held a sheaf of papers in his hands and was singing to a woman who sat on a higher platform a few feet from him. Though her back was to me, I knew at once who it was because of her beaded red hat with a black feather.

E turned slowly toward Stephen. She, too, held some papers—a script or some sheet music—and was turning as if to answer his song. I hadn't heard his words, but I was not about to miss her response. Her voice was thin and high. It was completely unlike her speaking voice which was commanding, strident, and confident. Truth was, she couldn't carry the tune unless the tune was purposefully off-key. There was a look on her face, though, which showed her to be happy. I had seen her satisfied, I had seen her laughing, but I'd never seen her happy. Her face was magnificent in the light. She sang:

> I know what you're trying to say to me
> I know you think you mean what you say
> But you don't believe me when I say this to you
> You'll be gone when the night meets the day
>
> So go back to the boys in the squadron
> Go on back to the work that you love
> When night meets the day you'll be dressed all in blue
> And I'll be blue as the mourning dove

E punched out every word in the first two lines of each verse and softened her eyes and voice for the last two. It was pure cornball and I loved it.

When she finished, E and Stephen looked over to my left. Apparently William Casten had been seated where I couldn't see him through the door. He approached his players, wearing his three-piece suit without coat. William was jubilant and clapping as he came up to Stephen. "Excellent, perfect!" he cried. He squeezed Stephen approvingly on the arm and headed to E, clapping again as he walked.

E was standing after her number. She and William laughed with each other, hooked their right arms, and spun around twice, square-dance style.

Never mind that I was the child outside the party. This was magical theater and I shared the moment. I also sensed that their rehearsal, or whatever it was, was over. I exited without fanfare.

That evening at the foundry marked the last time I saw E Baker.

Two volumes support each other over in the literature section. One is index and companion to the first. A man wrote the original work in seven years; a woman compiled her criticism and analysis in two years.

His head and his heart lived in his volume from the first sketch. When the book was finished, he climbed in all the way and stayed. A book is a house, and the builder's soul is always the tenant. This builder stayed to enjoy each winter's fire.

She discovered his plan and learned his limits. She pinpointed each stud, counted the nails, and logged in the nuances. She looked in at the window, measured the carpet, rattled the doors and tested the structure. She watched it bear wind and rain and some cold, and then she presented her flawless, uncanny companion prints. With her work passersby could understand why the roof tiles curved just so and the windows worked well without shutters.

Before she compiled her critique, she had written her own novel. Hers demanded no analysis or codebook. It was solid, hardbound, and stood its ground well, but quietly, far away in the contemporary fiction section.

He probably didn't read hers, didn't need hers, to finish his work of seven years. He never met her or thought of her as subject, object, puzzle, or author. For her part, she hadn't needed him to write her own novel, but she did need him later to convince her publisher that she could produce marketable and serious work. She needed his coattails to help her buy the boxes, books, grapefruit, biscuits, beans, bifocals, carbon, and those other things from which her life was assembled.

He and his work sit on the shelf. Her work keeps him up there, in place, while she is working on a second set of plans of her own or driving to a neighbor's home.

Where's anything about my guinea pig and how fast does a spider bite?

YOUNG CUSTOMER

CHAPTER

14

February 1

Dear Matt,

I spent a week not far from you. Could you tell I was nearby? I stayed in Mt. Dora, and I saw several of the store's customers while I was there. I never realized how many people drive to Chapters and Verse for a browse and a read. A couple of them looked at me like they knew me but couldn't match face, name, or place. I decided that I was like a landmark to them—recognizable and welcome when in place, but nonsensical and of little relevance when somewhere else.

I'd like to live in a small town like that. Show me some oak trees and a relative absence of malls, and I'm an easy mark. Besides, I've discovered that the smallest town has, to some degree, everything you can find in Tangelo, Orlando, or even New York. If it has a bookstore or library, it should not be missing anything.

Sneaked a picture of two teenage boys teaching themselves to dance in a garage. Such determination could bring world peace if everyone had it.

I'm between Edgewater and Boca Raton as I write this. Send some money to the Boca address below to welcome me there. I've got sweaters to buy.

Us old people do get cold,

E

Sometimes it seems that there's a book on everything. In our computer section, we have books on buying computers, selling them, cleaning them, programming or upgrading them, talking to them, listening to them, overcoming them, loving them, and even singing with them. Our literature section has books by Poe, biographies of Poe, critiques of Poe, historical novels about Poe, stories of Poe's alleged drug use, a picture book of Poe's Baltimore haunts, and somebody's monograph on Poe as a reincarnated Old Testament prophet. Nobody's ever asked for a book of puns using Poe's name, but somebody has probably written Poe Substitutes by now.

Still, people ask for books which just don't exist. Authors in search of new subjects should eavesdrop around bookstore information desks to learn about these holes in the market. I keep a mental journal about those unwritten books which I think will sell and try to suggest them to my author friends and to visiting publishers' representatives.

To begin with, there is one entire segment of the reading market which is overlooked—the truly incompetent. There are plenty of books for people who want to develop this or that skill, overcome shyness, or determine their strong points. But what about the person who can't parent, can't start a business at home, can't flatten any part of the body, and can't say yes or no comfortably? There are millions of people out there who can read but who can't do much else. They need books to tell them they are not alone—novels with incompetent heroes, murder mysteries with "important clue" or "he's lying" in parentheses here and there, recipe books for meals you can buy in the frozen-food section—something!

We could sell those books. We could also sell quick reads about racquetball-playing detectives, a series for young adults on a pair of teenage clairvoyants who play electric guitars, travel books on the cultural side of Anaheim, Las Vegas, or Orlando, and detailed guides to interstate-highway rest-stop selection.

Evan says the problem is not that authors aren't looking for subjects which are not yet explored in print. "Most authors quickly realize when there is an unfilled 'niche' in the market," he says. "They also know what books a portion of the reading public wants them to write. Publishers know it, too, and when the two parties find each other, there is a book in the making. No, the problem is not in finding things to write about or publishing books which some people will want to read. The problem is in finding things to write about which matter. These are left to authors who feel that their subject is more important

than its place today in the market, and publishers who dare to print
books which many people did not know they needed to read."

I say we can sell those and still move books on the lives of
spouses of television stars or on cooking with chocolate.

Of course I knew E had been nearby; I had been the
audience that night as she sang William's song. I had no idea
why she hadn't visited the store or me, why she had stayed
outside of town, or whether she planned regular visits. If
anyone was privy to her travel plans, it was not me. This
thought hurt a bit, but I decided that her brief return had
something to do with the foundry and nothing to do with
visiting old friends. I continued my detective work.

We have three hardware stores in Tangelo—three and a
Sears. I figure if every child, woman, and man in town needed a
new power drill at the same time, there would be enough for
everyone with dozens left over for visiting cousins.

This apparent epidemic of hardware stores may seem
unnecessary in our small town, but it's okay with me since
shopping for tools is a lot like browsing among bookshelves.
The variety is great, and every special-purpose wrench, every
specialized ratchet set or clamp assortment is the product of
someone's creativity. A purchase of a tool or a book is both a
nod of respect for its creator and an act of communication.

Ramsey Wills owns one of the three hardware stores. His
store is called Hodges and Reese, after two men Ramsey admired
as a boy and wanted to honor. When I came in, Ramsey was
reading the book Thad Collins had bought for him. I had to
interrupt him. "Hey, Ramsey, can I ask you something?"

"Just a minute. Have you read this? Listen! 'No matter what
happens today on its surface, the land itself will endure.' Now
that's nice. Does it mean anything? What do you need, Matt?"

"Some information."

"Information? Listen. At some point you need to buy
something from me so I can buy something from you. It's called
balance of trade."

"Okay. I do need a spreader, but see, if it works right and
the fertilizer makes my lawn grow, I'll have to mow more often."

"You got it—more mowing, more blades, new spark plug,
new mower. Then I can come in and buy that book on young
poets I've been wanting. Balance of trade . . ."

"It's a deal. Next spring. Ramsey, you're the only guy in town who sells surveying equipment, right?"

"Right. Hodges and Reese has a certain exclusivity in that department."

"Who usually buys that stuff?"

"Most all of it is special order. I think I've only sold it to maybe a half-dozen people in the last year, and most of those just wanted the small accessories to finish off the equipment they already had."

"Anybody buy the basics recently—the tripods and sextants and all?"

"They're not called sextants. They're surveyor's levels and yes, I sold two of what they call starter units to the county."

"Anybody else?"

"Not in the last year, and I probably won't sell any more for a good while."

"Why not?"

"Because it's almost closing time.

"Ramsey, why won't you be selling any more?"

"Because I rent them out now."

"Ramsey, I've got a book for you. It's called *Country Wisdom—When to Keep It to Yourself Because It's Getting Too Cute.* Now. Who has rented the starter units?"

"An appraisal agency over in Deltona and E Baker."

"Why E Baker?"

"She asked. In fact, renting was her idea. She didn't say what she was surveying. I thought she was putting the stuff in her window and told her that it didn't do anything for my business when I tried it. She brought it back in two days and I think she might actually have used it. She also bought some stakes and red plastic flag tape."

I looked at the surveyors' tools he had on display. "Ramsey, what do you see when you look through the telescope on the surveyor's level?"

"That things aren't where you think they are. Something to do with the curve of the earth . . ."

The book about the old man and the pearl and the moon—I need it.

YOUNG CUSTOMER

CHAPTER

15

Certain people need certain books. While I am usually canny about these critical needs, I cannot prescribe books as a doctor does some chemical remedy and be reasonably certain that the prescription will be filled or followed. In fact since "needed" books almost always would jolt their readers into new worlds, they are rarely read.

But, if I could prescribe for some of my regulars:

Patient: *Tommy Weintraub*

Diagnosis: *Transplanted New Yorker who still feels the South to be crass, shallow, and generally undercultured.*

Rx: Look Homeward, Angel, *any Eudora Welty or Walker Percy. Heavy dosage until series is completed.*

Patient: *Liddy Pennington*

Diagnosis: *Absolute faith in the benign rationality of governmental action and of humanity in general.*

Rx: Salvador *or* Johnny Got His Gun. *Take both at once for maximum effect. Do not take on an empty stomach.*

Patient: *Louise Sampson*

Diagnosis: *Chronic addiction in its advanced stage to trash fiction, a condition associated with fear that "serious literature" is beyond her.*

Rx: John Cheever *for ease of passage. Take in weekly doses to permit prescription to slowly enter system.*

Patients: Bill and Diana Sumners

Diagnosis: Deep-seated belief that the rich have a lock on nobility.

Rx: The Stories of Breece D'J Pancake, *all of Jamaica Kincaid. Do not take with expensive wine.*

Patient: Howard Knight

Diagnosis: The poetry left his life thirty years ago.

Rx: Far Tortugas, *some Denise Levertov. Repeat application as often as necessary.*

The business side of me knows not to recommend these certain books to these certain people, because they would be upsetting and because it is an unwritten rule of retailing that store clerks avoid personal involvement with customers. The mischievous and know-it-all side of me demands that a way be found to get the right books read by the needy reader. Both sides have been known to claim victory.

I suggest that everyone prescribe books for their friends. However I do have a vested interest here, just as a doctor has in keeping some sick people around.

March 3

Dear Matt,

Two weeks in a Daytona hospital weren't on the itinerary. They wouldn't let me take pictures inside, either. I surrendered my camera to someone called the hospital purser and noticed on my bill when I left there was a purser charge of $25.50. The hospital cashier assured me that my insurance would pay 80 percent of that fee since the claim form would record it under "Laboratory and Holding Fees." I've decided to avoid all income taxes from now on by calling my payments from you "Laboratory and Holding Fees" and writing them off as expenses.

So do not hesitate to send my March fee to the Boca address. I got the February check when I finally arrived (feeling fine, thanks for asking) and now can use another to pay for an overpriced efficiency. I haven't seen a bookstore here yet, but I know there must be one. As someone said about somewhere, though, it's hard to find the here that's here. (Maybe it was the there that's there, and maybe it was Gertrude Stein, but I don't have a literature section across the aisle so I can't be certain.)

Did the spring lists come in yet? Anything big? How are you doing with "that" exercise book?

William says you're very dependable with your Thursday visits. I wish I could sit with you two while you have those talks he calls your "late-night decaffeinations."

I've never thanked you for the notes you've been including with your payments. If I ever seem crusty and uncaring, you should remember that I miss the place, the people, the rows of friends on the shelves. Your news is read and reread so I can imagine the little adventures I know you're enjoying every day.

Your wandering predecessor,

E

Sometimes you just need books. As a boy, I could take them under the covers, knees up with a flashlight, and escape from the trials of childhood into a chenille-walled adventure cave. I fed Oliver Twist and struggled to help Robinson Crusoe until the batteries ran out or I was reminded of my bedtime hour. In high school books told me what adults could do with their lives, what some people thought was beauty, what themes were to lace the rest of my years, and a bit about death. I still see books as personal friends and teachers, even now when I must also see them as inventory to be turned over five or six times a year.

Books turned on me only once. I was one of those students from the South in a northern college. My southern accent helped me often because most people there, students and professors, associated slow talking with lack of intelligence. Imagine someone from Mobile understanding organic chemistry, or some tall fellow from red-clay country reading Garcia Marquez!

While my accent helped me catch my colleagues by surprise, my weak southern education worked to make things difficult. I had coasted through high school, partaking of the hardest courses until my last year or two when the courses ran out. Two years of yearbook, typing, chorus, enrichment, student assisting, and class government were fun at the time, but calculus, more foreign language, and a remotely intelligent jab at physics would have been more useful when I hit college.

Since advanced studies weren't available, I staggered a bit when I hit a heavy course load and classes full of prep schoolers who snoozed along with an "I've had this stuff before" advantage. I ran scared. Books, which had always been my retreat, began to take on a different role.

At the beginning of each term, as each course reading list was distributed, I'd carry larger and larger stacks of books back to my room. During the term these stacks seemed to grow and shift about on my desk. Finished books took to the upper shelf on the wooden bookcase attached to the back of the desk. Books to be read inched their way up the line from the bottom shelf formed by the desk itself. The middle shelf was where books would breed. This was where the "supplemental reading lists" made their presence known. I took these seriously, although I think I knew that virtually no one else bothered to buy or read these extras. I had ground to make up on the northern students.

So each term found me huddled before a wall of volumes, a forbidding wall whose bricks I hadn't gotten to pick. I kept a few thin volumes next to my bed for "the real me" (Ferlinghetti, Frost, Farina) but rarely looked at these friends.

It was sometime in my junior year when I conceived of the telereader. One night, in my desperation to read all the supplemental texts, required articles, assorted approved readings, and the like, I realized that the operative imperative, as we were wont to say in those days, was not to read at all. The goal was to prove to the assigning professor that we had read.

We could read, reread, take notes, summarize, and review, but if we didn't confirm our efforts with correct responses on essay tests, we would not be rewarded. I wanted to be rewarded, and so I created the telereader.

At that time, students were packed off to college with a few essentials, like a high-school graduation dictionary, a Smith Corona portable typewriter, a few dollars with which to open their first checking account, some stationery from hopeful parents, and an invention called the Tensor lamp. The Tensor lamp made its living by concentrating, and thus was a natural for students. It also got incredibly hot as it focused its light of knowledge on page after page of Russian history, astronomy, or Sherwood Anderson. I remember one classmate whose Tensor burned him so often that it became an object of terror in the dormitory and eventually the subject of an impromptu play called Invasion of the Killer Tensors. Entire armies of these lamps, gawking and shining from the stalks above their mysterious, white-hot black-box bases, attacked Richmond, Virginia, for the heinous purpose of melting the statues on Monument Avenue.

100

I had a better use in mind for this villain of heat and concentrator of light. I pictured a special bulb which, when substituted for the normal hundred-thousand-watt Tensor bulb, cast a radarlike beam in the space between my eyes and the pages of the book in front of me. As I read, the light would color the words on the page, much as a highlighter would. A completed book would thus be completely colored, probably in yellow. Why not, I reasoned, hand in this yellow book to the professor interested in my reading and thus offer proof of my efforts?

The special, channeled deviance of the college student's mind took over. Why should the professor believe that I had read the book when I could have just colored it in? Simple. A Tensor decoder would be used by the professor to determine if the marks had been caused by mental effort or just coloring, which could be performed by any fourth grader or freeloader. How would the professor know which students had understood or concentrated on the parts of the book he most valued? I reworked my telereader's black box so that it could color in red the areas I reacted to most strongly.

At this point I was ready to develop a new industry. I didn't want the conventional task of producing or marketing the tele-reader itself. No. I decided that the real money was to be made in preread books. I would sell editions of Moby Dick, for example, with theme elements teleread in red for students whose professors were certain the whale was more than a bully. I'd sell another edition of the same book to students who were reading the book for professors who loved to analyze Ahab. I could cite, in red, obscure passages which would leave the professor wondering what the student, who obviously had read the book and savored the passages about Ahab, saw in the book that the professor didn't. I could even show the depth of a student's emotion about certain passages by burning a hole through the page. I debated a "genius edition" which would find the book covered in a pale, pale yellow wash, as if Evelyn Wood herself had speed-read through it. One or two summary sentences, or phrases, would be highlighted in medium yellow as if the genius reader had grudgingly noted the few words with any wisdom in the book.

The academic industry would first try to counter my preread book scheme by placing seals on new texts, but I knew that I could get the used-book-exchange owners to sue them, and win, on a restraint-of-trade claim.

Eventually the professors and other forces of evil would develop a thought-print detector to determine whether the thought prints which had caused the highlighting on the book submitted by each student could have been created by that student. I'm sure I had a counter measure for that, but today, so many years later, I can't remember it.

I do believe that, used honestly by the student, the telereader could eliminate a great deal of testing and leave more time for teaching and learning. On the negative side, libraries would have the yellowest books in town if people used the telereaders. The libraries would fall into disfavor. Then again, people would just have to buy new books in order to read privately.

Business? Buy low, sell high. That's business.

CORB SAMS

CHAPTER 16

Robert James Porter is in, carrying four copies of that book of his. Robert James is not so bad, I guess. He's just like the rest of us, sticking his face into the wind and offering up what he can of himself. Maybe the difficulty I have with him is that his face is around too often in places I'd rather not see it. Maybe the reason I'm uncomfortable around him is because he reminds me of Arnold Watson.

Arnold is a fellow I met at college. He was older than most of us there and, in fact, had been an adult for a while before going back to school. Being older, he was accepted by the rest of us as uniquely qualified to bring the outside world into the classroom, to keep the professors honest, and to inject reality into academic discussion. In those years we pleaded for relevance the way we now plead for a break, so Arnold had lots of fans.

Looking back, I'd have to say that he cultivated an image of experience in a calculated way in order to establish his special credibility. He was totally successful in this regard, and thereby introduced me to one of the more dismaying features of American culture.

Arnold was from a West Virginian settlement just north of, and somewhat smaller than, Lizemores. His home area had no real name and, he claimed, no remaining inhabitants. Arnold told us stories of ghosts in his hollow and of primitive cures for earaches. He told us of a tiny town to the southwest with a tunnel entrance and ongoing feuds. As we sat in our comfortable classrooms, he described his two-room school and the footbridge he had rebuilt daily in order to reach it.

Arnold parlayed such stories into all kinds of honors. At least twice a week, he left campus to serve on a board somewhere. He was on advisory boards of other colleges, governing boards of several Washington-based, nonprofit agencies, and publication boards of three academic journals. These appointments—forgive me, Arnold— didn't come to him because of his brilliance. Arnold was selected because he had been born and raised in a place so authentically Appalachian that it had no name. He reveled in talking about his background and selected his tales from among the most romantic. People liked Arnold and had a need for him: Arnold became a professional hillbilly.

Thanks to Arnold Watson, I began to identify a small subculture of men and women who, by virtue of their age, race, sex, nationality, religion, or other accident not of their doing, gained positions on committees, boards, or councils. Many of these folks were abetted in their rise by laws which required that "at least one-third of the governing board shall be made up of persons whose parents may be certified to have lived at least four years in confinement in a Baltic state between 1935 and 1975," or some similar selection criterion.

The phenomenon of professional Indians, older people, urban priests, and the like fascinated me. At one point I even submitted a satirical paper to my Current Political Aberrations seminar describing a mythical agency called the DOA, the Dead Person's Office on Advocacy, an agency which championed the rights of the one silent majority which was always forgotten and whose voices were never heard. The professor rightly cited my crassness and completely ignored my clever selection of the agency's governing body.

Robert James Porter marks the latest evolution of the Arnold Watson phenomenon. Robert James Porter once wrote a book. It was a bad book and no publisher liked it. Robert James was not disheartened. He borrowed from his mother and published the book himself. He brought it to me to sell. It did not sell, but Therese put it in a window on Florida books once since it had a shell on the cover.

Robert James took pictures of the window. He used the pictures to wrangle a speaking engagement at the Friends of Longfellow Society, which was a dwindling group of friends who had moved to town together some thirty years earlier from Longfellow, Indiana. Through the years they carried on as if they were interested in poetry, thereby qualifying as professional poetry readers. For their monthly meetings, they sought out anyone remotely connected to literature who would speak for free. Robert James Porter qualified on both counts.

Having published a book and made a speech, Robert James Porter printed business cards reading "Robert James Porter, Author,

Lecturer, Generalist." With these solid credentials, it was easy for him to get speaking assignments and spots on local panels about this and that cultural matter. With each panel or lecture, his résumé grew more impressive until he became, at long last, A PROFESSIONAL PERSON. He's working now on a second book about life in the public eye.

March 15

Dear Matt,

Thanks for your concern. No, I'm really quite fine. "Stable" is the term the doctors used last. I've always been too stable, in my opinion.

I'm beginning to understand something about the American spirit at my advanced age. When all the fooling is done, there are only three good ways to go through life. The first is to search yourself for the greatest of your gifts, develop that gift, and give it as often and as beautifully as you can. The second is to decide that your best effort is in living a life of daily example and contribution: the good family person, hard worker, teacher, community supporter. The third is to make total peace with yourself and live any damn way you want which doesn't cause any problems for anyone else. Our society rewards all three approaches.

Maybe we booksellers take a fourth path: we give other people's gifts.

Sorry for the philosophy. You're stuck with it because this isn't the usual business letter but a midmonth thank you for your note. Besides, I have lots of time to think just now.

Here's some business for you. About four years ago, we ran a spring promotion on home fix-up books. It was very successful, as Therese and Evan will remember. However, when I looked at several of the books we were promoting and noticed that most of them used only males between thirty and forty-five in their pictures, I swore we'd never repeat the promotion. I never relented, out of stubbornness and a desire to punish those offending publishers who don't know how well this woman handles a radial arm saw. I'll bet they're still smarting from the lost business.

Last week, I looked through four new do-it-yourself books. Each of them showed only hands doing various jobs—

unisexual, ageless, colorless hands. I say, start the promotion at once. You'll see Therese and Evan smile when you suggest it. Just promise you won't tell them it was E's idea. Speaking of tools and their use, I have to tell you, Matthew dear, that while you have every right to ask me why I used surveying tools at the old foundry, I have every right to keep silent on the matter. No offense, but didn't you know that I try to answer every personal question with a question of my own? Besides, a writer will tell a reader what the writer wishes to tell. The reader has the pleasure of filling in the holes.

I'm beginning to enjoy letter writing. You can think before you speak in letters so you always feel more clever. Red cheeks don't show, either. Too bad there aren't many epistolary works around now. Encore, Helene Hanff!

Most sincerely,

E

The hardest days are when I'm tired of people. These are the days when everyone seems selfish or just predictable—accusations which may be true sometimes but which are nevertheless unfair. Still, sometimes, everyone is intruding.

I long for the sun on the cold lake, fire and flannel, fresh food, fresh coffee. My mind runs for an upstairs corner room in a white frame house, somewhat chilly, overlooking the lake, overlooking the quiet. Up in that room, I would cull the hopes and turn them this way or that to catch the sun off the lake. I'm sure that I could, if I could get away, light up the hopes and shine them like lanterns in the rooms of those a little short of hope of their own that day.

March 18

Dear Matthew,

About that letter I wrote you a few days ago—the snippy one in which I told you to mind your own business when it comes to my real-estate activities: it's been bothering me since I mailed it.

I apologize. It is none of your business, but I should have been more diplomatic in saying so. I have this image to protect.

To make reparations, I will make the matter your business, like it or not. You did ask.

It's William. He has dreamed for years of putting on his musical. He works on it all the time, growing it like a garden with a sampling of every known flower. Last time I asked, he had sixty different characters in it and seven scene changes.

It may be impossible by now to stage the thing. I don't know since I've only read parts of it, but I do know William Casten and I believe that he lives for his work and wants to see it performed.

We all have someone whom we'd like to please or emulate, even if we never tell them. William is such a person for me. By the time you are his age, or mine, things aren't supposed to happen to you much, and you're not supposed to happen to them. He has taught me that living means trying to be an exception to that rule.

Savory Characters keeps him going, and I want to help him see it performed in full before he dies. So, roundabout, I get back to your question and the surveying.

Before I left, William and I often ate together. When we drove here or there, looking for a different restaurant, he would always point out buildings or scenery which seemed to fit his play. "That back room would be perfect, perfect, for the scene in the union meeting hall," he'd say.

Once, when he came by to pick me up in that old Chevrolet that he has no business driving, he saw the foundry building. It was just the place for his play. When we went inside, he saw that it had a large room and started converting it in his mind for the full performance. "We must draw a floor plan for the stage and block the major scenes on paper," he said, "but we shouldn't touch the room until we can get a crew in here to do it right." He wanted to rehearse in one of the foundry's smaller rooms. He has drawings for the large one, the theater itself, in his office.

Never mind that the place was falling apart, had holes in the roof, no parking, and probably wasn't safe enough for the fire department to approve its use by the theater-going public. William, in his mind at least, established the Foundry Play-house. I am certain he could envision every chair, every seat number on every chair arm, every board on the stage floor.

He wasn't concerned that someone else owned the old place. He knew it would be perfect. That left me to try to get it for him.

As you know, I've never owned any buildings or land myself. I've always thought it curious and arrogant that people would try to own a piece of the earth. I am most ignorant about such matters and found myself discussing property with the one person who is ignorant about nothing— Corb Sams. "Buy now, buy right," he said. He also offered to put a down payment on the property in his name, since I didn't want to let William know what I was doing. For all the bluster, Corb is an intelligent, understanding fellow. And discreet.

Corb talked to the owner, a man in South Carolina, and got him to hold the property for us. They didn't exactly settle on a price—the man didn't promise to sell at all—but the owner did promise not to sell to anyone else. I gave Corb some money (actually it was your money, thank you) and he developed some sort of legal agreement that gave me three months to raise the rest should the man decide to sell.

I knew that no property changes hands without a survey. Since I've always wondered what those people with their yellow tripods and hand signals are doing out in the middle of the road, I decided to survey the property myself. I got two books on how to do it, took a three-day class at the community college, and rented some instruments from Ramsey Wills. Corb helped me and we did a fine job—deserve an award for it. It's not official but it is right.

What I learned isn't good. There is no property around the building to speak of—three feet on one side, six on the other. You can't build a driveway around back, and there are only fifteen feet to the front road. NO PARKING, as the signs say. That means, according to Bella Craddock at Town Hall, NO THEATER unless the foundry is torn down and rebuilt smaller.

William doesn't know any of this. I don't think he needs to. I'm hoping he finds another place just as "perfect for the production." Meanwhile Corb says I'll probably lose the original payment. That's not important. My worry is for William. He's not all that young, as you know, and there are only so many possible theater buildings in Tangelo.

Now that you know, you are a potential accomplice. Where might he stage his play? Any ideas?

I don't like these long letters. Too involved. It's easier behind the counter. People come in, tell their tale quickly, and they're gone. For the moment, I'm gone as well. Don't worry about any of this.

Yours without a snip,

E

The brokers keep appearing. Most businesses probably hear from them from time to time so I shouldn't let them bother me, but they do. It's not that they're hard to turn away. Most of them clearly don't "have a client quite interested in buying this business" but just want a listing. It's not that I think they or their clients would take financial advantage of me. Small, independent bookstores aren't exactly candidates for buy-out attempts by corporate raiders, and most, like mine, aren't worth much more than their inventory. No, the problem with brokers is that they live off quitter's temptation. Clean starts are always appealing.

It is entirely honorable in business to take the money and run. An offer to buy your business may be treated "like any other business decision." Make the right profit, determine the optional uses of the money you'd receive and the money you've tied up in your business, and the decision almost makes itself.

There are certainly days when I could be entirely honorable in this way. These are the days when:

1. *Water stains appear on the ceiling above the para-psychology shelf.*
2. *The parcel-delivery company changes drivers, and we get somebody else's Quik Start spark plugs instead of our sure-sell forty copies of the newest Robert Ludlum thriller.*
3. *Remains of an ice cream cone are excavated from beneath the Young Adults section.*
4. *I realize that no one has sent me flowers for over two years.*
5. *I realize that I haven't sent flowers to anyone for over three years.*
6. *I think of all the things E would do better than I can.*
7. *The bank balance ends its sixth straight week in the red "but I know I can cover it with Saturday's and Sunday's receipts."*

109

8. *I look around and can't find anything to read.*

The code words for brokers are "I've never really considered selling." That means I'm in a business mode and already negotiating price.

*I used to like books about rockets and old presidents,
but not anymore. Do you have any just stories?*
YOUNG CUSTOMER

CHAPTER

17

*National news rarely worms its way into
the conversations of our staff or customers.
People may be concerned about the presidential
debates, the strength of the dollar, or congres-
sional squabbling over the national debt, but they
don't dwell on these matters once they get inside*
the store. The U.S. is but one shelf on the wall in here.

An unlikely exception to the insularity of the store from hard
news came with a news release from the space agency. It had decided
that it was okay for private companies to blast the ashes of the dead
into space to remain in eternal orbit, as long as launch safety was
assured. The government should know that Tangelo bookstore types
think the idea is outrageous.

Therese, who is not usually interested in governmental doings,
came in on the morning of the announcement enraged by the idea.
She waved the paper with its headline, "SPACE BURIALS OKAYED
BY U.S.," at anyone nearby. "I don't want my loved ones circling
about every three hours. When they're dead, they're dead. How can
I overcome my grief if they spin by all the time?"

Lawrence was positively grim when speaking of the idea.
"It's no mistake," he intoned, "that the president unveils a military
research proposal that will lead to destruction in space in the
same month that the space agency says it's okay to bury people
there."

Evan was astounded by the audacity of private enterprise and
the willing complicity of the government. "My tax money will now
pay to see that someone else's departed departs safely, and then, no
doubt, we'll all pay to monitor the orbiting crypts to see that the
departed stay safely departed."

I stood with the others against the idea because I remembered another intrusion into our skies. Years ago, when we had the old Strategic Air Command base near here, people would look up and some would tremble when the huge, silent, high-flying shadows called U-2s would pass over. As a boy, I felt the fear that boys of earlier times must have felt when introduced to the awesome destructive capacity of a cannon or a Gatling gun. There was something evil about having such power in the sky. At other times the sky was the best of my friends. I studied the clouds on winter days while lying on my back on our sloped driveway. I named the different blues over Tangelo: everyday royal, deep black-blue, blue of secrets, and every once in a while, prophet's blue. A U-2 had no rightful place between me and my blues. Neither do someone else's relatives, even if there is a special ash-compacting process in the works.

To vent our staff's frustration with the project and the anger several of our customers voiced about the proposal, we resorted to a contest. It was a clever little game which I was secretly hoping would get some national attention. We asked our customers to "Name that Celestial Tomb." The first and only prize was a silver flight jacket specially emblazoned with the only arm patch we could find—a round one reading Future Mechanics of America. To enter, customers had to write opening lines for a novel about the pioneers in the program, or write a book title for such a novel. Puns were encouraged though not required. The winning entry would be read aloud every three hours for a week, or until we grew tired of reading.

Response to the contest was much like response to all our sales gimmicks—limited. We got seven entrants, of which six were book titles:

When Mourning Becomes Electric

The Importance of Being Urns

David Copperfield . . . David Copperfield . . . David
    Copperfield

Grave Blue World

Gone with the Wind: A Capsule Version

Space Burial: A User's Guide

The one entrant who offered opening lines gave us an opener worthy of many best-sellers:

"John, I told you to label all those cans before we loaded
    them. It's not right sending up unmarked six-packs."

We never announced a winner. The jacket is hanging in my office, slightly used from our window on The Right Stuff. *Nobody noticed that no one won.*

May 21

Dear Mr. Mason,

I understand that my sister, E Baker, used to write to you on a regular basis. If that is true, you must be at a loss to explain the lack of correspondence in the last six weeks. I'll tell you what I know of her activity in this period and would respectfully ask that you do the same for me.

E wrote to me from a Daytona hospital in mid-February. She rattled on about the architecture of the hospital and its unusual billing practices. She didn't say a word about her condition, except to tell me that she was being medicated and that her doctors seemed too quick to seek a radical solution to her problem.

By the time I called the hospital, she had already been discharged. They would not tell me, her only sister, the nature of her illness. I was told she had left a publisher's office as her permanent address. Since the publisher is in New York, and E planned to stay in the South, I was naturally confused. I had to assume that she had left the only address she could, having sold her business and given up her home. I think she should have kept her home since everyone should have an address of her own. She didn't and wouldn't agree.

E wrote again at the end of March. She was packing to leave a small town called Boca Raton to take photographs in Tavernier. She said she had read something about the houses there being built with special techniques to withstand hurricanes, and she hoped to photograph master builders working with apprentices on these unique constructions. I didn't hear from her again until she called two weeks ago.

I scolded her, perhaps too harshly, for not letting me know where she was for so long. E said she wasn't sure herself where she had been since she left the hospital in Daytona. That worried me, as you may imagine. I convinced her to come stay with me and she agreed. She has never agreed to stay with me before. My household is a bit too proper for her, I believe. This time though, she said she probably should rest with me for a time and promised to leave at once for my house in New London.

She hasn't arrived yet and I'm quite concerned for her safety. I went back through her letters from the last several years and developed a short list of people with whom she corresponds in hopes that she is in touch with one of them. A polite, busy young man named Evan Taggert told me you were on vacation, so I'm writing you, hoping you will call me when you return.

I am terribly worried about my sister. I fear I will see her on national television any evening now. Knowing her, she'll be standing with the president of these United States, lecturing to him about how to prepare his memoirs for most interesting reading. Like the old joke, one reporter will turn to the other and say, "Bob, we know that is E Baker up there, but who is that man with her?" At least, if that scenario were to take place, we would know where she was.

Have you heard from E? I called her publisher, her attorney, and a friend she and I have had since grammar school. No one has heard from her lately, and I'm afraid I've upset everyone I've called.

Enclosed is my calling card. Please telephone me when you return so we can share information and perhaps find my sister. My hope is that she has been sidetracked by something "just right" for her book and has become totally engrossed in her work. She does that.

Most sincerely,

Margaret Day Baker-Pierce

I'm looking for a book about a family who moves out of the city to where they don't know anybody and nobody wants to know them.

YOUNG CUSTOMER

CHAPTER

18

We get our share of strangers here. As they do in most towns in our state, tourists arrive, drink in our sun, comment on how clean everything is and how friendly people are, spend too much money, and move on. Like most Floridians, we welcome these visitors, try to keep out of the sun, rail at taxes levied to pay for new roads, congenially take the tourist dollar, and stay put. It's a balance with which everyone seems comfortable.

Since tourists are, more or less, a cross section of the rest of us, a certain percentage of them are readers. Too many seem only to read road maps or vacation guides, but a good number let books go along on their travels. A special few even include bookstore hopping as part of their trips. Members of this last group are called saints.

Just about everyone who lives in town has been past our front counter at some time, so I figure that anyone I don't recognize is a tourist, a visitor of some sort, or someone from a nearby town. I like them all instinctively. They've already proven themselves to have good judgment by their very entrance into Chapters and Verse. Everyone knows that a bookstore frequenter is a more interesting person than, say, a barhopper, whose literary interests are limited to the daily horoscope. Everyone knows that.

These new people are liable to ask for anything. I remember one man who wanted everything we had by Wallace Stevens. He said he couldn't learn enough about Stevens and was on his way to Stevens's home. We didn't have anything by Stevens alone but did find him in two anthologies. Our visitor snapped them up and headed north on his long drive to the literary shrine he assumed would exist in Reading.

115

I enjoyed chatting with this man and remember his comment that Stevens, an insurance-company executive and a poet, was as close as the U.S. had come to a Renaissance man in this century. I wanted to press my case for Einstein or Archibald MacLeish, but my customer felt so good about his man that I stayed quiet.

We had a British family in once—two parents, one boy, one girl, pink cheeks, navy clothing, genuinely pleasant. There was a contentment about them and one characteristic I find extremely rare among us 'mericans. They were totally unconcerned about the impression they might make on anyone else. They were not in any way inconsiderate; they were simply self-contained and comfortable as a family. This trait, coupled with my helplessness before a British accent, made me think that we'd cornered the perfect family. When the children bought Charlotte's Web *and discussed how they'd take turns reading the chapters out loud, I wanted to applaud.*

I've been conscious of my reactions to new customers for some time. I'm not sure what to call these people. I can't call them strangers since strangers are, according to common usage, male only. Writers are to blame for this, since they always mean men when they evoke mysterious strangers, dark strangers, howdy strangers, or menacing strangers. Lots of our new customers aren't men, so I tried the thesaurus. Outsiders, newcomers, and jackaroos aren't appropriate for obvious reasons and aliens aren't looked on too favorably, so I'm still without a term. Whoever these folks are, I like them and continually overestimate them.

I was worried. E hadn't written for six weeks and hadn't shown up at her sister's as promised. She had disappeared, reappeared, and disappeared again after admitting that she could not remember where she had been.

I missed her monthly letters and was holding two of her monthly checks, waiting for a mailing address. Perhaps she was ill again, somewhere. I worried that she had collapsed, been taken unconscious to a hospital, and remained in a coma. It seemed quite possible that no one who knew her was aware of her situation. She could be a Jane Doe to the hospital staff and might need someone to make life-and-death decisions for her.

After receiving the letter from Margaret Day Baker-Pierce, I decided to ask William Casten if he had any idea of E's whereabouts. Before lunch I walked over to the hotel.

There was no conference at the Windsor that day. Instead the WELCOME VISITORS TO THE WINDSOR letter board offered the modest message, "Complimentary Coffee." I say take the compliments when you can get them, even if they're from a cup of coffee.

"You're looking good this morning."

"I like your suit."

"Nice grip."

William was behind the front desk, working the morning shift. To a stranger he wouldn't have appeared to be the owner of the hotel. An owner wouldn't be working the desk and, if he were, he would somehow find a way to let the guest know he was king of the castle. "Owner's ego" is what I call it. I know it well.

William greeted me as if he didn't recognize me. "Good morning and welcome to the Windsor," he said.

"It's me, Matthew," I said. Then I realized that his eyes had been closed when I came in.

"Of course it is," he said, shaking my hand across the front desk. "Welcome to the Windsor, Matthew Mason. A little early to be arranging the books, isn't it? Or have I dropped an afternoon somewhere?"

He began to talk about what was on his mind. Darkness was what he talked about—not darkness as in *Heart of*, not darkness in the souls of men, just good ol' black darkness. This man loved it. He said it was the only thing that made people enjoy the day, and that we should welcome it. Darkness and quiet were inseparable to him, and he said that both were what let people listen to themselves.

"If we had true darkness, we could listen so amazingly well," he said. "The perfect situation for composing a musical would be in a dark room, sound and smell proof, where you used no colognes and you wore soft shoes so you couldn't even hear your own feet shuffle."

He smiled and looked around the lobby as he envisioned this room. I thought it sounded terrible, like the absolute darkness the cavern guides brag about before they turn out the cave lights. I wanted to ask him about E, but I knew he would have to work through his concept before he'd move to the next subject. "Doesn't that mean that the perfect composer would be blind, deaf, and without olfactory senses?" I asked him.

He liked that idea. "Yes. Blind and deaf to those things which keep the rest of us from writing music that is miraculous.

We are always interpreting, comparing, taking direction. If we were locked away from the outside for a while, locked in that little dark room, who knows what we might find inside! As we surprise ourselves with our own ideas, we can flip on our desk lamp, a little pin of light in the dark room, and put our private voices on paper."

William had been turning a small card over and over in his hands as he spoke. When I realized that it was the same calling card I had just received, I nodded toward it.

William stopped talking, looked at the card and then looked at me. "Ah, E's sister has contacted you also. That's why you are here, isn't it? Given the worries of Miss Margaret Day Baker-Pierce and yourself, I suggest we try to find E. I haven't heard from her myself for some time and would like to be assured that she is being her irascible self somewhere not too distant from us."

"Any theories on where she might be?" I asked.

"No theory, but a starting point. Perchance you are available this evening for a drive of approximately one hour?"

Perchance I was.

Travel books aren't about travel any more than novels are about other people.

CORB SAMS

CHAPTER

19

"... I got to get jalopies. I don't want nothing for more'n twenty-five, thirty bucks. Sell 'em for fifty, seventy-five. That's good profit. Christ, what cut do you make on a new car? Get jalopies. I can sell 'em as fast as I get them."

Why would I remember these lines? What makes me look up a few lines out of thousands and thousands I read fifteen years ago in an American literature course? Did I think about these lines then?

Steinbeck's used-car salesman in The Grapes of Wrath wasn't talking about books, but we've got our jalopies at Chapters and Verse. These are the novels which people buy, read, forget, give to the library sale, and maybe buy again. I see it over and over. Somebody picks up some generic novel by some unknown author, realizes that he or she has an adequate read to look forward to, and another jalopy leaves the store.

Winifred Pugh reads jalopies like so many other customers, and who's to question her taste? Certainly not this happy bookseller. However, Winifred Pugh doesn't understand that even these novels have human authors, and few humans boast long rows of published novels of whatever quality. She continually asks us to order more books by her favorite authors, even when they are dead or are no longer being published for lesser excuses.

To be honest, I've sometimes shared her frustrations. If Faulkner cared about me, he'd find a way, even now, to write a sequel to As I Lay Dying. Frank Conroy should write his autobiography again. Anne Tyler could write a book a month, and Annie Dillard could assemble those spare, wonderful sentences much more often; I'd still want more. I'd stand in line all night to buy something else by Cervantes.

119

Although we were in the front seat of an automobile, driving with William Casten was more like driving a motorcycle with a sidecar. This person, this appendage, was exposed and vulnerable—completely trusting and dependent on my own driving habits and the whims of the other drivers on the road.

We were riding in his car. He had insisted that we take it since it was his idea to find E. He had also insisted that I drive because he hadn't driven more than five miles at a time since before he had taken over the Windsor. His old Chevy, a 1953 model, drove heavy and smooth and didn't seem to care that I was driving instead of William. It ran like new and had a comfortable feel like the Windsor.

William directed me to the interstate and headed us east toward the beach. We weren't ten minutes out of Tangelo when he reached into the back seat to get a long, flat box he'd brought along. With my worries about E and my curiosity about where we were going, I hadn't asked him what it was or why he had brought a box at all.

William opened the end of the box and pulled out an electronic keyboard. I'd seen instruments like it before, mostly larger ones used in rock bands. His was the kind with a hundred levers and choices. It could play carillons and cymbals, violins and oboes. I had tinkered with one like it at the department store. It had something called "Human Voice," which I would have played except there had been no power hooked up to the floor model.

William set the keyboard on his knees and clicked on the power. He had the thing set on "piano" and the sound wasn't bad. Neither was William's playing. I didn't recognize the melody and, when I glanced at his face, I could see that William didn't always know where it was going, either. He was playing along, entertaining himself.

His music was jerky, sometimes repetitive, but full of humor. He glanced over from time to time to see if I was listening and to read the response on my face. At one point he played in the highest octave, tickling the highest notes over and over like a feather tickling a child's chin. That started both of us laughing.

"This song is called 'Low Budget Toys,'" he told me as he kept playing. "In the show there is this family which has no money. The father is continually entertaining his daughter with

120

sight gags and dolls made of shadows. In this song he's doing that old trick where he passes his hands over his face from top to bottom, changing from a frown to a smile and then reversing himself. You can hear him do it right here in this part. There."

I could see the father and daughter. "What happens to the family?" I wanted to know.

"I'm working that out now. But I can give you an idea. First you have to know the theme of the show, so let's talk about themes. Back when, we were all told that there are only three themes in any art or literature—man against man, man against nature, and man against himself. Thousands of English teachers peddle this nonsense every year as truth."

The interstate exits flashed by as we continued east.

"There is, I believe, but one theme in all of art and this is it: Man must try to make sense of it all before he dies. The rest is diversion, passing time, keeping busy enough to dodge the question of why. We're all bundles of curious atoms. *Curious Atoms*—maybe a sequel to *Savory Characters*—eh, Matt?

"So that's my theme and that's what the poor family is trying to do. They have no choice. The only thing in their hands is to decide how happy or dismal they'll be as they try to make sense of things. I've decided they'll be happy. Listen."

William moved several levers on the keyboard and set two other switches. Chords began to accompany his melody and he started a new song. "Dining on Sunshine," he whispered to me so as not to interrupt his own playing.

After a few moments, William began to sing. He didn't really sing all the notes but sort of spoke them in the rhythm, occasionally lifting or dropping his voice to where it would have to be to carry the melody. His simple lyrics brought us both to the breakfast table where his poor family ate only sunshine before heading off to work in the morning.

"I'd love to see your play," I said when he finished.

"So would I," William said slowly. "It will always need improvement, but right now I just want to know how this one episode will turn out. There isn't much more to do on the whole thing, though."

With that, William closed his eyes and put his head back on the headrest. I kept driving, looking over from time to time at him, asleep maybe, with these songs and dreams swirling about him. Meanwhile I just clunked along on the ground, worrying like a fitful piece of prose about how much gas was in the Chevy, where we were headed, and E Baker.

Just outside of Deltona, William awoke, played a simple melody, again in the highest octave, and turned to me. "I could stand with the best of 'em once. I was as tall or taller than most of the boys, and we'd laugh and play through the afternoon. That was when any future to us was maybe an hour away. I loved it then when my step was sure and my reflexes were that of . . . of a young animal.

"Funny how all that time, when I was one of the best of those boys, seems like a single afternoon now—a great afternoon, to be sure, but a single, small set of hours. I'll bet I've carried and worried that time as smooth as my grandfather's pocket dollar that I'm still carrying.

"I don't know who those boys were anymore. I forget the faces and the names. What I'd like is to see the face of my grandfather when he received the dollar from his grandfather, and on back in time until there were only boys and fields and rocks. I'd like to go back to where life was done with a spear and a fire; I'd be happy just hefting and turning the sweet, wooden smoothness of the spear in my hand. I'd like to go back to where I could sing as loud as I pleased to the sky and not stop sidewalk traffic or bring out the authorities."

I listened and drove further east.

"Did you know I have a brother, Matt? He's younger than me, but I always thought he'd die first. He was always old. Not unpleasantly old but never young. Last year, he slipped into his seventies without any strain. It was easy for him, I think, because he'd been practicing seventies rituals for so long. Careful, careful days. Every step under control. Diet, walks, calm. He's practiced all his life to be seventy, so it has been easy for him. The truth is, Matt, he has always practiced not standing up to the days and has learned how to let them wash over him without being disappointed. Do you have a brother, Matt?"

"No, just a mother, an aunt, and a cousin."

William was quiet for a few minutes. I supposed he was thinking about my nonextended family.

"And a bookstore," he said. "You and E have that."

An old cowboy—gray hat, worn vest, no gun—approaches the Lone Ranger, who is sitting on the edge of the sheriff's desk explaining to the sheriff the proper way to capture three crooks in a canyon. The Lone Ranger looks up, stops talking.

The old man nods at the masked man of justice and smiles. The Lone Ranger studies the old man's face and says, as always without expression and sounding as if he has a cold, "Flapjack McElhenny, the one man I never caught."

Flapjack nods: "Before I die, I want to tell you how I did it." He describes his fantastic hidden-horse trick and then, with a smile, returns the loot he pilfered some thirty years before. The two men shake hands and the old man leaves.

It's always seemed to me that successful criminals should come forward right before they die to explain how they did it. What's the point of doing something new with the various props and backdrops if you don't tell someone about it so it can be admired?

Every good author is an outlaw and therefore bound to reveal his forbidden deeds or thoughts to those of us who haven't been able to cross the line ourselves.

Why don't they put the author's address in the front so
I can write a book back to her?

YOUNG CUSTOMER

CHAPTER

20

"There it is, Matthew! The hospital! Turn here. That's where we're going. It's Spanish or Moorish or something Mediterranean—the perfect backdrop for a scene in which LeeAnn goes on holiday to escape from her troubles. I can hear her singing as she sits near a fountain in front. Maybe it's that song about the olives."

William had this way of imposing his play upon virtually any building, or perhaps it was that the buildings shaped his play. I didn't know which was true, but we had reached the Daytona hospital, and it was evidently the place William thought might lead us to E.

I hoped she was not inside, but I still worried that she'd become ill and had no choice but to be taken back to this place where she'd been treated earlier. When I reminded William that E had spent two weeks here in February, he assured me that she couldn't be a patient now. "She never travels the same road twice," he said. As an amateur student of her life, I wasn't so certain about that.

Inside, the halls were narrow and there seemed to be no windows. We entered one of the side doors and wound our way, after several wrong turns, into the lobby.

A cheerful volunteer at the information desk asked how she might help us. William said she had already helped us by the gracious way in which she had greeted us and, by the way, his name was William Casten. She took an immediate shine to him, the charmer. I was too impatient, however, to listen to these two get acquainted. Soon, I knew, William would begin talking about his musical, so I took command. "We're looking for a patient named Baker," I said.

"A Baker, I see," said the woman, looking through a computer listing of patients.

"No," I said, "E Baker."

"It's not a Baker?" she asked.

"Not A Baker, E Baker, a she," I said.

"What's Mrs. Eebaker's first name?" asked the volunteer, still helpful.

"E."

"Eh?"

"E."

"Oh. I see."

"So, is she here?"

"No. We do have a Baker, but he's a T. R. Baker."

"Do you have any women here who are unidentified?"

The woman looked at her printout for some time. "I'm afraid I don't know how to look up the unidentified patients. I haven't been trained in that."

William's eyes sparkled. I knew he was composing some song for LeeAnn—"Lost in Daytona With No ID," perhaps. He leaned over the counter until his eyes were only a foot from those of the woman.

"Might there be a way, my dear, that we can learn if our Miss Baker has been a patient here recently? Perhaps there is a records division or an intake department that could help us."

Happy to finally have a way to be of assistance, the volunteer directed us to the patient registration office and suggested we speak to a Juanita Helms. When William explained to Juanita that hospital staff had identified her as the only person who would know what we needed to know, she happily looked up E's file.

"Yes, she was here for twelve days beginning February 8 of this year. Of course I can't tell you why she was here, but she was discharged on the twentieth without any outpatient treatments specified at this hospital."

I wanted to know more. "Could you tell us what illness she had? She's missing and that might help us find her." I knew Juanita didn't want to tell us but reasoned that she might if she felt it to be in E's interest.

"No. I can't tell you."

"If I guess it, will you tell us? Was it a heart problem, a broken limb, amnesia?"

"I can't tell you."

"Well, could you tell us what illness she didn't have when she left?" I hoped my cleverness would be rewarded.

"She didn't have terminal pregnancy." Juanita was developing hospital hostility.

William realized what was happening. After a short pause, he said quietly, "I wonder if we might see the floor where she stayed. Had we visited her then, we might have gone right to that floor. What floor was that?"

Addressing William only, Juanita said, "Four. That's psychiatric."

We were both bothered by this news. E was unusual, sometimes even bizarre. She was pushy, opinionated, often domineering, sarcastic, impulsive, and intense. She seemed to laugh on a schedule all her own. However she was always completely rational and responsible, even when she might have wished herself to be whimsical or wild. E was no candidate for psychiatric services.

As we headed for the fourth floor, William laughed. "Wouldn't you like to be the doctor examining E in this situation?" he asked.

"And why do you wear that hat with the grapes on it?" I asked E on behalf of that hapless doctor.

"Scuppernongs are in season just now. Doctor, how long have you had that habit of twirling your pencil around inside your ashtray?" William answered on E's behalf.

The elevator opened on the fourth floor and we walked straight ahead to the nurses' station. By now I had learned that William could get the information we sought quicker and with more style than I could, so I let him lead. He immediately found a nurse who had access to E's record of care during her stay. This woman assumed that, since we were this close to where E had been, we must have authority to ask about her condition and get answers. She hadn't been on the floor during E's stay so she read and interpreted the chart for us.

"Patient complained of severe pain in upper right side of abdomen. (We get the stomachaches up here on four when there's no room down on Intestine Row.) Suspected gallstones or cholecystitis. Patient unable to give complete family history but stressed no shortage of gall in lineage. Blood work ordered, ultrasound scan performed. Gallstones confirmed. Cholecystectomy (that's removal of the gallbladder) indicated. Patient reluctant to lose gallbladder but relented and signed release with handwritten notation below signature: 'If my gall disappears with my bladder, I'll sue this place to get it back.' Doctor's notation: 'I doubt we could get it all if we tried.'

"Successful surgery on February 10, measures to protect against infection successful, bile flow restored to normal. Intravenous feeding for three days, light fluids, etc., etc., all normal after the operation. Patient remained additional, let's see, ten days. Doctor Hamlin recommended two additional days in hospital but patient insisted on discharge. Bed rest at home and a sixty-day convalescence recommended by discharge team to patient. Discharge nurse noted: 'Patient is less interested in her recovery program than in who wrote and published our pamphlet on rehabilitation. She insisted that she could take care of herself and that her body simply would not dare further treachery. Discharge team tried unsuccessfully to obtain phone number or address of patient or a responsible third party.' Patient was discharged on February 20, leaving in own vehicle. Medication prescribed for pain . . ."

William hadn't spoken during the nurse's recital of the facts. When the nurse finally looked up, he said quietly, "I dearly wish I could have been here with her. She'd have had flowers and song."

We had a regular, Linda Travers, who used to come in with her family. She always arrived after dinner, and usually with her daughter, Sarah. Her son and husband would sometimes come in at the same time, and sometimes wander in later, asking Linda if she'd had enough time to look. Linda bought travel books and novels by British women. Sarah stayed with the romances in our young adult section, although she occasionally strayed into American History and once bought two books on the Louisiana Purchase.

Linda died of cancer two months ago. She was a quiet woman and not much was made of her early death. I believe, however, that the craziness and sadness of her death hit everyone so hard that there was simply little to say.

Sarah and the men didn't come in again until today when they came in together. Sarah's father and brother browsed at the magazine section while Sarah went to her favorite haunt. Every few minutes one of the men would glance down the aisle to make sure that Sarah was still there. They didn't seem anxious to leave and never asked Sarah if she was ready to go. Instead father and son seemed to be silently shepherding the last of their treasures.

When Sarah arrived at the front counter, it became obvious that she had her own money to make her purchase—a new circumstance.

"It's good to see you again," I said. I wished I had words to speak for a town full of people who knew what a struggle Sarah and her family were undergoing. Still these were the first personal words I'd spoken to this thirteen-year-old.

Sarah began to cry quietly. I immediately felt guilty and was looking around for her father and brother when Sarah asked, "May I tell you the last thing I heard Mom say?"

"Of course," I said, realizing that she'd been storing this up.

"She was lying real still. She had stopped crying a few days before and was trying to make us feel okay about how she felt. All of a sudden, she looked at me like she did when I said something too adult for me. Then she said, 'I want to know what will happen to you. I want to know what will happen to me.'"

Sarah and her family left.

William had been wrong about the hospital leading us to E. Although we knew that she was traveling one gallbladder lighter, we hadn't learned anything to help us locate her.

I knew from what the nurse had read to us and from E's letters that she must have driven to Boca Raton from the hospital. I doubted she had rested or conformed with any of the other convalescence directions. "What now?" I asked William when we were back in his Chevrolet.

I need three books on water. Bad. By tomorrow.
                                              YOUNG CUSTOMER

CHAPTER

21

OUR CHOICES occupy a small section near the checkout. Since many customers ask for our recommendations, and since each of us on the staff likes to foist his or her favorites on others, we set up OUR CHOICES to help satisfy all parties. Each of us can keep three books in the section and nobody likes to give up a slot. Go on vacation and you can expect that someone has grabbed some of your territory in your absence.

Lawrence regularly rotates his selections between short-story collections he favors and P. G. Wodehouse. Evan keeps at least one Robertson Davies book on his roster and uses his other two spots for the last two books he's read. His excuse for such a nonselective approach is that anything he's chosen is his choice.

Therese's choices are the most eclectic. Today her contributions are a book on the Memphis school of design, a humor book about young British gentlemen, and Madame Bovary. When they sell, she might well be promoting a biography of a French general, an adult coloring book, and a collection of poetry by A. E. Housman. I don't know if her tastes vary that greatly, or if she feels she should offer something to every type of reader from time to time.

I take my own choices very seriously. I want to suggest only those books which I feel it would be criminal to overlook. Like two fans discussing which shortstop was the finest they'd ever seen in their entire lives, including that guy who used to play for the White Sox in the fifties, I debate my selections with myself. I'm looking for waterfalls.

Waterfalls are nature's best literature. Wherever they are found, they radiate life, power, purity, beauty, and inspiration. Like the great books, it is not possible to focus on anything else, or even hear anything else, while close to them. They are eternally in place, eternally in motion, and eternally willing to share themselves. They are also masking their greatest gifts behind a façade which is itself wondrous. If a book is beautiful and valuable for its technique, its language, its plot, or its characterizations, it is rare enough. If it involves its readers by beckoning to their souls, it is working miracles. A waterfall's technique and language may be seen in the play of light on the falling water, the clean spray that is always building along its front, and the demanding, unique thunder created by the water hitting the catch pool at the base. Its plot and characterizations are evident in the water itself. Calm, unsuspecting, it slices its way along a river or stream until at once it finds itself in air, separating, plummeting down without warning at faster and faster speeds toward its inevitable collision below. Changed, it can flow again.

Only a few books can create this drama. Fewer still are those which dare the luckiest of us to venture deeper and enter a world that no man could have purposely created. Behind the waterfall, inside the great books, there is a pocket of perspective in which the outside beauty is recognized and honored, but its inner workings are revealed as the real wonder. The noises are louder; there is unspeakable tension which forbids long stays. There is a view of the outside through the eyes of an author who has found astonishing beauty in the stone and water of every day.

It was nearly eight when we left the hospital. I wanted supper and suggested that we drive to the beach and eat on one of the benches along the boardwalk while we decided what to do next.

William agreed. "The hot-dog places close at sundown," he said, "but there's a pizza place a couple of blocks off the beach which will sell pizza by the slice. They'll put pineapple and pecans on it. I could eat that now. Are you a pizza eater?"

I couldn't even guess how William knew about this place, but its specialty, Polynesian Pie, was excellent. William drank a beer with his. We sat on a bench in the breeze, under the boardwalk lights near the pinball place. In front of us, the ocean made its patient gray noise. From behind we heard the bells and pings in the arcade. The breeze made a cool peace between them.

"William," I said, "where do you think we might find E?"

"I don't think we can. I was certain the hospital people would know. If they did, they couldn't tell us. Now E herself will have to let us know where she is."

"Are you worried about her?"

"Of course. Neither of us has heard from her in weeks and that's not like her. Still, if anything bad has happened to her, we'll find out soon enough. If not, we'll find that out also. E Baker is not a quiet woman."

"You saw her when she was in Tangelo, didn't you? Why didn't she stop by to see me?" I wished I didn't have to ask either question.

"She did come in for two days. She didn't say for sure why she wouldn't go by the store or call you, but I think I know."

"Yes?" The breeze felt colder; I was sweating.

"She has said before that a bookstore like Chapters and Verse is like any other work of art. It can bear but one artist. Another's hand would take away the direction and confidence in the work."

"She didn't want to overshadow me?"

"It was more that she felt that one signature is all the store needs. It may be, though, that she didn't come in because she doesn't have what you have now—the stability, the identity of that place. It might hurt her to see what she's lost so soon after she decided on her new career."

I finished off my pizza and turned to look at William. "I saw you and E and Stephen working on the musical at the foundry."

Some teenagers came out of the arcade, laughing about their adventures on a machine called "The Southern Tornado." William listened to their bragging as he considered what I'd said. "Did you like it? Which song did you hear?"

"Yes, I liked the enthusiasm. I only heard a bit of the duet about leaving before the night meets the day. What I don't know is why no one told me you were rehearsing like that. I would be happy to give a critique or read a part or just be an audience for you."

"We didn't think we should tell anyone because some people would think we were crazy. We do have these marginal reputations, I'm sure, and this activity would confuse a number of people. Watching E sing would be, for some people, like

133

catching a view of their parents making love. It might be a normal, wonderful thing, but behavior and belief over the years says it never happens. I see now that we shortchanged you by not including you, and I apologize. I apologize sincerely."

William offered me a sip of his beer and I finished the can for him. I looked down the boardwalk at the families and couples strolling in the evening. It was easy to imagine them breaking into song—a quiet, slowly building evening song about the wind and the moon. William's play might well be staged outdoors, I thought.

We let the ocean entertain us for another hour or so. We talked about E, speculating about the turmoil and wonder she would be generating wherever she was. Then, like two fishermen with nothing on our stringers, we headed home.

There are more days, now, that I spend entirely in the store. I come in early, eat soup for lunch in my office, stay late, and resent the occasional trip to the bank or post office.

When I took over Chapters and Verse, I worked some extended days out of excitement and fear. I was responding to the independence, responsibility, and the list of changes that would make things different under my ownership.

Somewhat later I took to fine tuning. I'd work some overtime to redesign our inventory system, fix sagging shelves, organize files, or whip an archaeology section into shape between History and Nature. I thought I might be a perfectionist and wasn't at all bothered by it.

In my next phase, I found myself coming in from time to time when there was no need. I came in to enjoy myself, to book shop. I loved the way the store smelled and how pensive people became once inside. I was a browser.

Lately I'm not sure why I stay in the store so many hours. It isn't because a great deal of work goes undone. I think it's the security of the contrived world inside that holds me. Inside is quiet, intelligence, humor, calculated tragedy, variety, and change I totally control. Outside there is the litany of world problems: danger on the roads, incredible waste in the schools, impersonality on the streets, cruelties of all sorts.

It's not agoraphobia. I'm not afraid to leave. But inside I'm safer, complete, and within these two thousand square feet, important. Sometimes I have a vision of my family and friends all assembled in the store for the night.

134

There was a problem on the interstate between Daytona and Tangelo. Two cars apparently had locked bumpers on the Sanford exit ramp and had spun around, side by side, facing the interstate itself from the shoulder of the ramp. With their headlights on, shining at those of us driving by, they looked like terrified animals, cornered and turned to face the predator. Gawkers were causing a slowdown.

William, who had closed his eyes just after we left Daytona, awoke when I slowed the car. "People are always willing to slow down or stop when they see something new," he said.

"It's instinctive," I said. "If you don't have something new to look at, your life whizzes by even faster."

"You're not supposed to know that at your age, Matthew."

The bottleneck ended after we passed the exit ramp and we picked up speed, heading the last few miles to Tangelo. William wasn't sleeping and he wasn't humming. I asked him when he thought his musical might be completed.

He laughed and then he grew quiet for several minutes. Finally he scratched his cheek under his eye and said, "It's not your fault, dear boy, but you can't know what you are asking."

No one had called me "dear boy" before, and no one but William Casten could do it without being condescending. I was proud to be addressed by him in that way, regardless of what I didn't understand when I had asked my innocent question.

"No one would want his work to be finished. Certainly not me. The fun is in adding to it. There's more to be added every day. More songs, more scenery, more actors—it's all building so nicely. Stopping it, well . . ."

He didn't have to finish. We were back at the Windsor.

> *Being solicitous to some people in the short run is shortsighted. Sometimes it is rewarding. If you want any kind of surprise, you have to try it.*
>
> E BAKER

CHAPTER

22

Irv Tyson and Corb Sams came in during the morning after my drive to the beach with William. Irv said hello and headed toward that shelf of doctor novels we keep almost exclusively for him—Evan calls these books "intestinal fiction." Corb began looking at the new arrivals next to the counter.

In a few minutes, Corb was reading loudly, for the benefit of anyone else in the store, some of the cover blurbs on the book jackets. "Riveting, scintillating, compelling, spine tingling, sultry, landmark," he read. "In the tradition of *Gone with the Wind*." Then he paused and announced that "any book about a war, a man, a woman, or even draperies will lay claim to being in the tradition of . . . Since when is one book a tradition anyway?"

"Corb," I said, "I haven't heard from E for some time and I'm worried about her. She wrote to me about how you are helping her buy the foundry building, and I was hoping that she had contacted you recently."

When I mentioned the foundry, Corb straightened up and returned the book he was holding to its shelf. He looked at me and announced, in his usual loud voice, that one should "never stick an exclamation mark in the middle of someone else's sentence."

That made some sense, and I realized at once that Corb was surprised by my inquiry. He walked to the front of the counter, directly opposite me, and leaned in toward me. Then he whispered, "Do you think E is all right? I lost track of her about four weeks ago myself."

Apparently Corb had not whispered in years, as he blurted his words out in a half-talk, half-whisper. As is the case with many other people, Corb's regular habits changed when E entered his mind.

He frowned when I told him about Margaret's letter and E's illness. "She called me once from that hospital in Daytona," he whispered with every third or fourth word spoken normally. "That was in February. She was complaining about gelatin, I think. I remember that she said it appeared once a day on a meal tray in front of her, as if laughing that it could shake about at will, while she was stuck in her bed with pain should she move about. I think she was medicated when she called, but who knows with E? We were working together on this certain project and she wanted to know of its progress. I really shouldn't say more about it."

I told him what I already knew about his making a payment to give E a chance to buy the foundry for William's play. My knowledge surprised him but, coupled with his concern for E, seemed to free him to talk about the foundry deal.

Corb explained that there were two groups besides E who were interested in purchasing the building. E's motive was known to us but not to the others. These others were two sets of partners who Irv had told Corb were all members of the Terrace Club. They each had spotted E surveying the site.

"Idle hands and upstairs windows with views of the town make idle speculators of idle men," Corb whispered. He explained that the two groups had smelled some development activity and suspected each other. Both had set out to determine who owned the foundry and the land on either side. Soon each group had contracted with a site planner to sketch a proposed project for the entire block, including the foundry. "One wanted to build something called The Renaissance. It was going to revitalize all of Tangelo with a shopping center, office buildings, and a condominium tower. Makes you want to stay unrevitalized, doesn't it?"

I agreed. "Did they buy up everything before E could get the foundry building?"

"No, but they started. They bought the three lots on one side, but when the other group learned about the activity, they went after the lots on the other side. Their project was called The Foundry Cityscape and was going to be a tourist attraction.

138

I think they were going to recreate an old Florida town which had never existed on the site, squeeze in some rides, and maybe peddle their own brand of Cityscape Chocolate." With his intermittent whisper, Corb sounded like a conspirator of the first order.

By now Irv was nearby and could hear those occasional words which Corb spoke aloud. "They . . . learned . . . side . . . attraction . . . town . . . chocolate . . ." Irv came over, to be able to hear better and to place a half dozen of his treasured intestinal-fiction samples on the counter. "Are we talking about the foundry?" he asked.

"'We' is an ever-growing number among rabbits and among people who claim to have read *War and Peace* but can't remember its plot," Corb responded in his familiar, loud voice. Then he returned to his uncomfortable whisper and told Irv, "Matt was asking me about E. She's disappeared."

"At least she has plenty of money," said Irv.

That surprised me since I hadn't sent her the last two monthly checks.

I thought of E in those few weeks before she had left. Maury Criswell had just left the store, having carried on for fifteen endless minutes about topics so inane that no one could have concentrated on his words for more than a few sentences. E muttered, "That man is sweet, but he is like this blank book here—he looks like a book and walks like a book, but he doesn't talk like one."

I looked at Corb, hoping he'd explain E's financial status but, for once, he didn't want to talk. Irv did. "She got a windfall. Mr. Corbin Hames Sams here is the principal cause of her good fortune. May I, Corb?"

Corb shrugged.

"When we were looking through the foundry, I told you that Corb had given the owner some money so that he wouldn't sell to anyone else for ninety days. The owner didn't promise to sell; he just said he wouldn't sell to anyone but Corb, who was representing E."

"I told E not to do that," interrupted Corb. "She was buying nothing really. She insisted though, and no one could have changed her mind with any argument we might consider to be logical and prudent."

139

Irv went on. "So here's how her stubbornness worked out: The time is almost up on the ninety days. There are only two weeks to go, in fact, and E is somewhere out on the highways. Corb here is twisting about, knowing E's investment is about to be lost. He's at a loss for what to do to save it."

"I'd prefer it if you'd retract that 'at a loss' description," Corb interrupted. "Why not just tell Matthew that I was reviewing all available options, seeking the best of many?"

"So Corb is at a loss, when he finds out that the two sets of partners have the property on either side of the foundry under contract. He senses opportunity. He ponders. He is no longer at a loss. Within two days both sets of partners mysteriously reach the same conclusion: purchase of the foundry building is essential to the successful completion of either The Renaissance or The Foundry Cityscape. They each know of Corb's interest, but they don't know what E has to do with the deal or about how much money is involved. All they know is that they must have the property and must get it before the other group. Corb becomes the man of the hour."

"There is nothing more dangerous than a man and his hour," laughed Corb. "I did shine just then, I must admit."

"So here is Corb driving in his station wagon toward his groves. Suddenly a car holding one set of the partners appears behind him. They follow him until he stops at the first grove. Next thing you know, they're all leaning against a maintenance shed, discussing how much money it would take to get Corb to sell his questionable option. The numbers have already doubled E's investment when a second car comes up with the other set of partners."

"First time ever for three cars together on Highway 109," Corb said. "Three farm kids from next to the grove came over just to count them all."

"Corb becomes silent. He knows what will happen next. Both sides begin to bid. Corb listens and watches like you would at a tennis match—a thousand more, a thousand and another, all cash, of course, all cash and another five hundred. Back and forth, back and forth, until both sides are fussing and eventually realizing that the numbers are getting out of hand. In true competitive spirit, the two sets of partners head off in a herd to the back of the shed to strike a deal."

"I waited like the child at his birthday party when his mother says, 'Now close your eyes,' and he imagines something big, red, and shiny being wheeled in. Something good was going to happen, and it was just a question of how good." Corb was smiling as he remembered. "You know what they said as they headed off to negotiate? They were talking about how there must be someone they called "a serious player" behind the scenes. Then one of them said, 'Now let Cal figure out what we should do. No one can blue-sky like Cal.' What could that mean?"

Irv interrupted. "The two sides agree to combine forces— maybe they'll make Renaissance Chocolate or run the water slide down the side of the office tower. I don't know, but they return with a final offer to Corb. By the time they left Corb at the shed, they had bought his interest out for five times what E had paid. The *Wall Street Journal* should have covered the negotiations."

"Are we going to get the office tower or the theme park?" I groaned. Cultural irony does not escape me. A Renaissance cannot be constructed on a single block in a small Florida town by a group of investors. Why, an earlier one took a couple of centuries and several countries to really get cooking. I don't remember any admission tickets being required in fourteenth-century Italy or any souvenir chocolate being sold, either. I was not excited by this instant cultural revolution here in Tangelo.

"Doesn't look like it," Irv said. "The foundry's owner refused to sell, so the old building sits right in the middle of the proposed entrance gates to the development. The owner did feel sheepish about keeping the original money, so he gave it back to Corb, who gave it to the partners. All the partners took a loss."

"Ah, there is more that you don't know," said Corb. Corb told us that E had not wanted to make such a profit on the arrangement. She was upset that she could not purchase the building for William Casten and wanted to give the profit back to the partners.

Corb had approached the partners with E's check but they had refused it. "Business is business," they had told him. "We may meet your backer again one day, perhaps holding the cards you held this time. Maybe we'll make the large profit then and we won't want to return it. Keep your winnings."

E had taken the money, Corb said, and had told him that she did, after all, have a good use for it.

One afternoon in those few weeks when E was teaching me about Chapters and Verse, I saw her standing next to the receiving table. She caught my eye because she was not moving, and I'd never seen her standing still in the store. She saw me looking at her and knew my question.

Her hand was on a stack of novels. "I've read all of these," she said. "Can you imagine what the authors must know about us in order to reach us as they do? You have to worry about the best of them for what they must know and carry around with them."

As Corb was finishing his story, I noticed that William was in front of the store. He had been headed inside when he was buttonholed by Robert James Porter. William was listening patiently while Robert James jabbered on, pitching away at something important to Robert James. The conversation ended with a handshake and William patting Robert James on the arm. When William he came in, he joined Corb, Irv, and me at the counter.

"Welcome to Chapters and Verse, William Casten," Corb said on behalf of the store. The three of us all looked at William with the same question on our faces and William answered, "He asked me to give every guest at the Windsor a free copy of his book."

"Would he give you the books to give away?" Irv asked.

"No, I'd buy them. Mr. Porter suggested that I raise the room rates to pay for them. He had prepared what he called a 'profit graphic' to illustrate his proposal."

"Would you do that?" Corb and I asked in unison.

"And cut deeply into the sales of my neighborhood bookstore? Of course not."

"It's okay," I said. "We've only sold four of the books in a year. I think every buyer had Porter for a last name. But you did something for him. Robert James went away, which means he went away with something."

"Well, we made a deal. I will place a copy of the book on the reading table in the lobby, and Robert James will provide a small, tasteful sign suggesting that the book be borrowed by our guests. If they wish to keep a copy, they will be directed to Chapters and Verse, which will be known on the card as 'the bookstore nearest you.' "

"You are a gentleman and a fine patron of the arts. You are also the soul of patience for talking so long with Robert James Porter, author."

142

"Anyone who dares take the risk to write a book of whatever quality deserves some admiration. More important though is that I learned that Mr. Robert James Porter has recently talked with our E."

"Where? How? Why Robert James?" Irv, Corb, and I asked these questions in sequence and all four of us laughed before William answered.

"Somewhere south of here. That's all he would say. I think he was using his knowledge for a bit of leverage in our negotiations about his book. My compromise only got me as far as finding out that he saw her about two weeks ago. I suspect he was going city to city hawking his work and just bumped into her."

No returns may be made by a thinking individual on the grounds that "I didn't like the book." Other individuals may return any book for any reason under our liberal return policy.

E BAKER

CHAPTER

23

The Windsor is spilling a small crowd out the front door. There are thirty or so people with silly, knowing grins on their faces, as if they've just been inspired in a conference to do something socially significant which they must do in anonymity. Each one carries a vinyl notebook; important missions must be organized.

As the initial party in the exiting horde gets closer to the bookstore, I'll learn more about their work in the Windsor. First I'll study the covers on their notebooks. Maybe a map of Florida, Georgia, and the Carolinas will become clear, along with the words, "Southeast Region, District IV, Camellias." I'll develop my initial theory that this is an environmental-protection group which has chosen to divide its members into numbered "action sectors" named after apparently harmless flowers. A silk banner with a camellia on it may drape their lectern back in the hotel.

With the initial group some fifty feet away, I'll have formulated a second theory, placing these people in an activist wing of a conservative political organization. This notion will be based entirely on my narrow-minded observation that each and every one of them wears leather-soled shoes. They're the Coalition of Rural Residents for a Better Country, and they've had six hours of lectures and workshops teaching them how to canvas their neighbors with a petition to provide additional tax breaks on land zoned as agricultural. Perhaps they are the Committee to Repeal Rights Bestowed on Criminals, and they've just received a list of judges in their areas they should work to defeat in the next election. No, they're the Council to Rate Regents Boards on Conservatism, and they've just developed, on flip charts, their new rating system. Emphasis was placed on a system easily understood by the media.

Now that they're only ten feet away, in front of Mo Samuels's empty storefront, I'll notice the lapel pins. Lapel pins either mean that the organization has been around a while (Sons or Daughters of some war, perhaps) or that some pin maker is a friend of the regional viceroy.

Maybe I'll notice that there are three colors of lapel pins, though each pin is shaped the same. Ranks. My theory will be revised once again, since the group obviously honors seniority or meritorious activity quite formally. Perhaps these are people who donate body parts. The kidney donors wear gold, the blood givers have blue pins, and those who wear the lower-status green pins are the ones who have promised their organs after their death, but have thus far given only a promise. People would talk more quietly to those with gold pins.

By the time the first wave reaches our door, I'll be sure of their identity and will have prepared for a hope-they-don't, hope-they-do invasion of the store. When the first hand pushes open the door, I'll be absolutely certain that the Windsor has not been hosting the Save the Greenbelters, the Change Resisters Reeducating Better Citizens, or the Transplant and Transfusion Providers of America. No, intuition will tell me that this is a group of Plexiglas distributors from the Southeast.

Intuition is only slightly aided by the knowledge that they've met at the Windsor every fourth Saturday for several years. Some of them buy books on personal finance, and one woman buys a book on opera or dance each visit.

May 26

Dear Matt,

Sorry I haven't written for so long. Another twist developed in my life which I hadn't anticipated. I always seem to check out for a few weeks when my mind's innards are in turmoil. I have learned not to communicate with my friends during those times because it would only frighten or anger them.

There have been few points in my life when I have been completely free to choose where I wish to live and what I wish to do. The first time this happened was before I moved from Connecticut to Florida. I spent weeks at home in Danbury, pouring through atlases, reading guidebooks, and preparing lists of characteristics I wanted to find in my new state. When I got to Florida, I spent three weeks trying to select a city and, more because I got tired of looking than anything else, I chose Orlando. Later, before I moved to Tangelo to open Chapters and Verse, I spent nearly a year making decisions about the right town, the best location for the store, and where I would live.

During all of these searching periods, I went into a "geographic stupor," according to my sister. I would talk of nothing but my quest for the perfect location and could think of little else. I would lose track of time and appointments, which is perfectly understandable to me, given the range of options I had before me. How difficult I must have been to be with during those times. (How mellow I have become. I must do something about that! Do not go mellow . . .)

After my stay in the hospital—one I would not repeat, as reading lamps shine differently when you are ill—I knew that I was once again going to make a change.

I missed the bookstore. I missed the bookstore life. I saw myself going from town to town, visiting bookstores in the guise of a traveling photographer, and I didn't like what I saw. I'm not a photographer. My name is E Baker and I'm a bookseller.

So, after four or five weeks of searching for the right spot, I'm opening a bookstore in Bryson Beach. It's warm here, pretty, and not as overbuilt as some places. I'll be a neighborhood store like you.

The funds for the new store flew into my lap by accident, courtesy of some brilliant financial footwork by Corb. I'm more than lucky to be able to get back to what I love. I can't be quite the size of Chapters and Verse, but Bryson Beach isn't Tangelo anyway. I am going to have a good nautical section, though, and at least a few shelves of everything. There's a staircase near the back which goes nowhere; I will use it for displaying up-and-coming authors.

I expect Willie Taragon to visit when he's not in Tangelo, so I'll know I have a working bookstore. He'll still have to drink his coffee outside, but we have a windowsill to hold his cup. I can ask him to report on your doings.

There is even a hotel nearby, though it has no lending library and no William Casten. It's one of a chain named for the color of its awning. The manager is a woman who has read everything ever written in French about lightning. She thinks that only the French have the character to understand why lightning is so jagged and sudden. You would enjoy listening to her.

About William: I believe you have gotten to know him rather well by now. He has written to me about your conversations. I want to ask you something. Do you think he might consider moving to Bryson Beach? I don't know quite how to ask him. There is a playhouse here which I've learned is always available for locals who want to perform, or who wish to rent the hall for the night. The group which runs it would welcome William. He could take an apartment near mine, and we could keep an eye on each other.

William keeps me young and keeps the fight in me, if you know what I mean. I'd dearly love to have him here. Would he leave the Windsor? I only wonder how he would react. Your eyes are always open to such matters, so I ask your advice.

The easy decisions about my new store have all been made—place, size, lease, and so forth. The hard part is at hand: I need a name. Help! My ideas are limited. Send yours. Mine:

1. Opening Lines—a little dramatic
2. Closing Lines—a little melodramatic
3. Letters—I like this one
4. READ HERE—I've always liked this one
5. E Books—may look like an eye chart on the sign outside
6. Bryson Beach Memoirs—might get me sued
7. Chapter 2, Verse 2—derivative, somewhat religious sounding, difficult to alphabetize in the phone book

You may have received a letter from Margaret Day Baker-Pierce. She hung up on me a few days ago when I called. I didn't contact her during those weeks when I was on the search which ended up here at Bryson Beach. She was mad about that, and because I didn't show up at her house as promised. She should know by now that I don't communicate well with my "old" world when I'm searching for my new one.

Margaret always forgives me for this one failing, but she was in a huff this time because, she claimed, I led her to embarrass herself with you in writing. She hung up and rushed off to try to retrieve a letter she'd just mailed to you. She had a right to be mad, but she's never understood how far out into the sea the strong currents take me. By the way, she's a wonderful sister and a good reader—mostly history.

The address below is the store address. I move in next Wednesday. If you want to take a week to help me order and set up, I'll waive my April and May payments. I'd love to have your help. If not, pay up, you scoundrel.

No. On second thought, I don't think you should come down until I've been open for a while. As you know by now, assembling a bookstore is an act of creation. I'm not a good choice for a collaborator so I'll spare you.

I very much like the idea that you and I are colleagues. Can two booksellers make a network?

Once again in the fold,

E

Back a few years when children were as pleased by basic electronics as today's children are by complicated video displays, you could go into almost any small museum and find what I called "light-match boards." Maybe one board would be a map of the state with lists of cities. You'd push a button next to "Amelia Island" and another next to where you thought it was on the map and hope the two right bulbs would light up. Another board would ask you to match up birds with their names, and still another lit up if you recognized your presidents.

Once I saw a man fixing one of the boards. He was turning it around to work on it and I saw that it was one with chemicals and their atomic numbers. I knew my chlorine and its Cl and wanted to give it a try, but I guess the bulbs were out. When he turned it enough so that I could see the back, I saw this maze of wires and solder, tangled in a scheme I couldn't trace. Every wire eventually reached a single battery. It was far messier, far more complicated, and much more difficult to follow than the bulbs it lit on the other side.

I can imagine E in Bryson Beach, roaming around READ HERE, building a special place which will change that town. I see myself up here in Tangelo and I imagine that there are people like E and me, behind various counters all around the world. William, Irv, Ramsey, Mo, Taylor O'Keefe, even Robert James Porter—we're all like those light-match boards. We're complicated, not so orderly, and the subjects and products we are able to deal with are limited. Still we're all connected to the same source of power and dedicated to getting things sorted out for the questioner.

As proprietor behind a particular type of checkout, I believe that if there is any hope for humankind, it may be that people who don't listen will read. That's a paradox that gives me comfort.

Most people I know engage in conversation only to exchange facts. When interpretation, emotions, opinion, or disagreement try to snake their way into a discussion, they retreat. As Corb might say, "Tell me, leave me." They have constructed a life and, face to face with someone offering a new set of blueprints, they simply don't get involved. If they are themselves ignored, well, fine. The world is peopled by thunderless herds of desperate ostriches.

Books are such clever creatures in this circumstance. They don't seem to talk back; they don't seem to look the reader in the eye and question motives or behavior. They can easily be made to go away. Books seemingly offer neither censure nor reward. If they do cause questioning or changes, few people can trace these back to a certain book or passage. What innocent little ostrich prods they are.

"Chapters and Verse, purveyor of prods. May I help you?"